*Within
the
Lighted
City*

The

John

Simmons

Short

Fiction

Award

University of

Iowa Press

Iowa City

Lisa Lenzo

*Within
the
Lighted
City*

University of Iowa Press, Iowa City 52242

Printed on acid-free paper

Library of Congress Cataloging-in-Publication Data

Lenzo, Lisa, 1957–

Within the lighted city / Lisa Lenzo.

p.   cm.—(John Simmons short fiction award)

ISBN 0-87745-611-9 (cloth)

1. City and town life—Michigan—Detroit—Fiction.

2. Detroit (Mich.)—Social life and customs—Fiction.

I. Title.   II. Series.

PS3562.E497W57   1997

813'.54—dc21   97-15908

01 00 99 98 97 C 5 4 3 2 1

for my mother and father

Contents

ACKNOWLEDGMENTS

I'd like to thank the following people for their guidance, encouragement, advice, care, and faith: my writing teachers, Charles Baxter, Stuart Dybek, Jaimy Gordon, Arnie Johnston, Jack Ridl, and, in memoriam, Dirk Jellema and Sandra Simon; my fellow writers, Bret Comar, Richard Hefter, and Jane Ruiter; all others who taught me and provided for me at Hope College and Western Michigan University; my editors, Barbara Bonner, Laurence Goldstein, and Mary Hill; all "The Quilters," present and past; my mother and father, Susie and Joe; my daughter Chloe; my ex-husband, Mark; and my brothers and sisters, Amy, Jen, Anthony, Marilyn, Sheri, Kris, Virginia, Peter, Jenni, and Steve.

I'd also like to thank Jaimy Gordon, Shirley Scott, and Western Michigan University for providing me with a generous fellowship; my mother and father for being my own personal matron and patron of the arts; and Cherie Giller, Jean Crawford, and the Saugatuck-Douglas Interurban Transit Authority for helping to make paying my mortgage with enough time left to write both possible and enjoyable.

These acknowledgments would be incomplete without special thanks to Stuart Dybek, who agented my first published story and has since recommended my work and me many times; his continued advice and encouragement in the years since I was officially his student have been indispensable.

Some of the stories in this collection originally appeared in the following magazines and anthologies: "Stealing Trees" in the *Michigan Quarterly Review* and *Sacred*

Ground: Writings about Home,
"The Angel Thomas" in the *Alaska
Quarterly Review* and *The PrePress
Awards: A Sampler of Emerging Michigan
Writers,* "Burning" in *Third Coast,* and
"Self-Defense" in the *New England
Review.* "Waiting" was broadcast on National
Public Radio through the PEN Syndicated
Fiction Project.

"Stealing Trees" is for Laurence Goldstein.
"The Angel Thomas" is for Stuart Dybek.
"Burning" is for Bret Comar and Richard
Hefter. "Self-Defense" is for Jaimy Gordon.
"First Day" is for my father and mother and
for Kris. "Waiting" and "Sophie's Shirt"
are for Jane Ruiter and Chloe and in
memory of Johnny and Steffie.
"The End of the Crackhead" is for
Peter. "Within the Lighted City" is for
Bret Comar, Stuart Dybek, and Jane Ruiter
and for my brothers and sisters.

Stealing Trees

We started stealing trees after the elms were dead and gone, when the city planted a twig in front of Frank's house. The twig had no branches and no leaves. It was as thin as a car antenna. From Frank's front stoop at dusk it was invisible.

So Frank and I started driving around at night and stealing thicker, bigger saplings, ones with branches and lots of leaves. We'd dig them up from the better neighborhoods in northwest Detroit, dump them into the trunk of Frank's Fairlane, and replant them on Frank's front lawn.

Frank refused to call what we did stealing; he was always correcting me: "Tree relocation, Stanley. The 57 Farrand Street Tree Relocation Project."

We could plant the trees at Frank's house because Frank's mother didn't live there and Frank's father never noticed what we did. Mr. Chimek played cello with the Detroit Symphony, and when he wasn't in concert he was upstairs in one of his rooms, either practicing music or listening to it. Occasionally he'd wander downstairs and fry himself some eggs, then go back up without turning the burner off. I can still picture him leaving the house for a concert: dressed in his black suit, white hair springing out of place, walking past the trees without turning his head. I lived five blocks over from Frank, and since my mother never passed by the Chimeks' house, she never saw our accumulating collection of stolen trees.

I suggested to Frank that we stop stealing trees after we'd bagged and replanted half a dozen. But Frank pointed out that stealing trees was less degenerate than setting tires on fire and rolling them down the ramp of the underground parking lot at Farrand and Woodward, something we used to do all the time in junior high. And by relocating lots of trees onto his front lawn, Frank said, and sneaking a few onto the lawns of our neighbors, we were helping to restore our city's reputation and name: "Highland Park, City of Trees."

We used to watch for the signs with these words—stamped in a circle around a tree silhouette—when we were little kids coming home from Detroit; crossing over the Highland Park border, we'd shout, "*Now* we're in Highland Park!"

In those days, the elms formed a ceiling of leaves a hundred feet up from Highland Park's streets. I didn't notice the leaves over my head as I grew older any more than people notice the ceilings of their houses. But when I was a little kid I used to look up past all the space to where the layers of green began and watch the breeze stirring the leaves and imagine myself up there.

Ten years later, there wasn't a branch or leaf left in all of Highland Park's sky, but the signs were still standing. We watched for them on our way home from stealing trees, and though we still spoke out when we crossed over the border, our voices were quieter and our emphasis had changed. Most of the time we'd be smoking a joint or a pipe. "Now we're in *High*land Park," we'd say. "City of *Stolen* Trees," I'd sometimes add.

"Relocated trees, Stanley," Frank would insist.

Daytimes that summer, Frank and I worked at the rag factory at Woodward and Cortland, cutting up new rags and washing and drying old ones for the guys at Chrysler. Evenings we played basketball with Frank's neighbors, usually quitting when it got dark, but when we felt like it playing on into the night using the light Frank had rigged on his garage. (The guys we played with said Frank should turn the light off and just use himself as a bulb, he was so pale—blond-white hair, moon-white skin—that he almost glowed in the dark. They didn't comment on my whiteness, except for once when I was sunburned, and Dwight Bates fouled me and I cried out, and Dwight said he thought all the tender white people had moved out of Highland Park.)

Besides stealing trees and playing ball, another thing we did that summer at night was sit around while Carol Baker cornrowed Frank's head. Cornrowing was big then, but just among black people. This was before Bo Derek.

I'd sit on Frank's porch and watch Carol working through Frank's hair and listen to her fuss and scold and threaten to slap Frank if he didn't hold still. As Carol got close to finishing, she'd swear she'd never braid such a fine-haired jumpity fool ever again. But Carol braided Frank every week all that summer, and whenever she went to slap him, her palm landed so lightly it was more like a stroke. Frank would reach up and take hold of Carol's hand, and Carol would pull away and threaten Frank some more. Frank just smiled and fingered his braids. He liked being fussed over, and the tight, close, pale braids kept his hair out of his face, which was perfect for playing basketball, and for stealing trees.

In August of that summer, Frank's father had a heart attack and died. Frank and I found him on the floor of his practice room with his tiger-necked cello lying beside him. My mom said Frank could come live with us for a year (we had one year of high school to go), but Frank wanted to stay where he was. He'd lived in that house all his life.

Two weeks after Mr. Chimek's funeral, Frank decided that we should steal a tree from downtown. He had seen its picture in the paper next to an article about the new Blue Cross building. The tree stood out in the foreground of the picture, a dome-shaped, leafy maple. So far we had stolen only locusts and oaks, the main kinds of trees being planted back then. The maple looked almost too big to steal, but we decided to check it out in person.

First we smoked some marijuana. Then we drove downtown. The maple looked even better in real life. Its hundreds of leaves were perfect and huge, and it looked as if its branches had been set in their upward, outward curves with a whole lot of planning and expertise. But there were too many cops cruising around down there—they never gave us a clean opening. At two o'clock in the morning we got on the Chrysler Expressway again, lit another pipe, and headed north, back toward Highland Park.

We hadn't gone a mile when Frank spotted the tree of heaven on the freeway slope. Later, planting the tree on his lawn, Frank said, "I've thought of another name for our project: the Otto Chimek Memorial Grove." But when he first saw the tree of heaven, Frank didn't mention his father, he didn't say anything at all—he just pulled over onto the shoulder and looked at me with his high, shining eyes.

"What are you doing?" I said.

Frank pointed at the tree.

"What?" I said. "You want *that* tree?"

It wasn't the best-looking tree even from the car. Just your typical ghetto tree that grows anywhere at all, but mostly in vacant lots and from between sidewalk cracks. Not the kind of tree that anyone plants, let alone steals. I looked at it, branches angling downward like palm fronds, then at the green sign hanging from the freeway overpass just ahead: MACK ½ MILE. On our trips between downtown and Highland Park, we had seen the sign plenty of times, but we hadn't even thought of stopping here before. This was a part of the city where black people didn't stop unless they knew someone who lived here, and white people didn't stop here at all.

The tree was growing close enough to the overpass that if a car crossed overhead we could hide below, and if a car came down the freeway we could scramble up on top of the overpass. I tried not to think about what we would do if cars came by both places at the same time.

Frank pulled on the hood of his black sweatshirt and tucked handfuls of his long braids inside the hood until none of the dozens of plaits showed. I pulled on my black baseball cap. Then we got out of the Fairlane and started up the grassy slope.

Old, dry litter cracked like glass under our feet. I looked at the overpass to my left and felt like I was on another planet. All my life I'd seen freeway embankments and overpasses, but never from this angle, the overpass at eye level, the embankment slanting under our feet, nothing between the overpass and us, nothing between the grass and us, but the cool night air. Standing on that hill made the whole world seem tipped and slanted—it seemed like the world had been set on its edge.

I spread the garbage bag beside the tree. Frank pushed the shovel in to its hilt eight times, cutting a circle around the skinny trunk. He had just got the roots separated into their own private clump when we heard a raggedy car in the distance, up on street level.

Suddenly it seemed a bad idea to duck under the overpass. It came to me that every movie that ended badly had people getting wasted in closed-in, concrete places. Frank and I glanced at each other. Then he ditched the shovel and I dropped the bag, and we ran the rest of the way up the slope and jumped out on the service drive and started walking along it as if we had not just run up there from the expressway canyon.

Soon we heard the raggedy car, or at least a raggedy car, approaching from behind us. We forced our breathing slow, tried to loosen our legs and our shoulders. The car drew closer, and then alongside us. We turned our heads toward the car but kept walking. The driver, black as the car's upholstery, leaned his head out the window. "Can you please tell us how to get to the corner of Russell and Pearl?" he asked, his voice a perfect imitation of a prissy white man's. Four or five others inside the car laughed. All of them were black. At least one was a girl.

Frank smiled in the direction of the carload of people, trying to act as if he were relaxed enough to think their joking funny. He kept walking. I kept step with him, wondering where we were going. We were getting farther from our car.

"You boys lost?" someone from the back seat said.

"No," Frank said.

"Oh yeah?" the driver said, sounding black this time, "You sure *look* lost." More laughter came from the others.

Frank glanced at the driver. "Yeah, I know we do," he admitted, just the right amount of blackness creeping into his voice—enough to let them hear that he was not a total outsider, but not so much that he seemed to be making any sort of claim. We still kept walking, but we didn't say anything more. It was better to say too little than to say something wrong.

"Where you boys from?" the driver asked.

This time Frank didn't answer.

I steadied my breathing. "Highland Park," I said carefully, trying to sound offhand and matter-of-fact, as if I didn't expect my answer to boost their opinion of us.

The girl shrilled something wordless from the back seat.

"Highland Park!" the driver said. "They let you boys stay in Highland Park?"

"For now, I guess," I said.

The driver eyed me more closely. Then he laughed, almost a friendly laugh, his lips breaking wide. He looked to be about twenty years old. He was wearing a light brown shirt zipped open at the throat. "And where you going later, man, when you got to move?"

"I don't know—*Romulus*, or somewhere," I said, with true dejection at the prospect. I'd never seen Romulus, but I had it pictured as rows of dirty white shoebox houses that collapsed when the jets flew overhead.

"*Romulus*," someone from the back seat said. "Where the fuck is *Romulus*?"

"I know where Romulus is," the driver said. He jabbed his finger in the air. "Shit, you got to move, man, don't move to Romulus. The whites out there so mean they don't even like whites."

"If I was white," the man in the passenger seat said, "I'd move to Grosse Pointe, Bloomfield Hills, somethin' like that."

"If you was white," one of the men in the back seat said. "Listen to the nigger: 'If I was white.'"

The three in the back seat laughed loudly and easily. I let myself smile but kept my own crazy laughter down in my belly.

"I got one other question to ask you," the driver said. The laughter stopped. I could feel all the ground I thought we'd gained slipping away from us. "Why was you digging up that tree?"

The trouble that had been floating around grew bigger and clearer, pressed at the quiet. My vision started shrinking inward, I couldn't focus, I could hardly see. I didn't look at Frank or at the driver or anywhere.

"I know there's plenty of them raggedy trees in Highland Park," the driver said. "So what I want to know is, what do two white boys from Highland Park want with a tree that's as common there as dirt? I mean, that tree is as common in Highland Park as niggers are, am I right?"

"We've been digging up all kinds of trees, from northwest Detroit, mostly, and planting them in front of his house," I said, glancing at Frank. Frank was looking down at the pavement.

"You boys really are lost," the driver said. "This is not northwest Detroit."

Frank kept on looking down. I couldn't see his eyes. Frank! I thought. Do something! Save us! Frank had a way of winning people over to him, sometimes without saying a word. Too bad this wasn't a carload of old people or women or girls. But even among the guys at school Frank was well liked, for a white person.

I thought of letting the men in the car know that Frank's father had just died. I thought of letting on somehow that he'd died just last week, just last night. But as soon as I thought of it, I knew it would be a mistake to bring up that subject at all.

"I don't think you boys really are from Highland Park," the driver said. "I think you're from one of them suburbs where they let the raggedy white folks live. Taylor, maybe. Or Romulus."

I thought of ways to refute this—name all the streets in Highland Park, show the eraser-burn tattoos our sixth-grade classmates had rubbed into our shoulders, at our request. But I thought that eraser-burn tattoos might be a Highland Park black thing rather than a black thing in general, and Frank's and my tattoos wouldn't have shown up that well anyway in the dark, being white on white.

In fourth grade, when our school was just about half black, the black kids in our class made plans to build a spaceship and fly to the moon, blowing up the earth as they left. They talked about it one day while the teacher was out of the room, said they wouldn't save a thing on earth except the people they took with them, and started calling off the passenger list. They named all the black kids in the room, and then one of them said, "And Frank Chimek." "Yeah!" another boy said, "Frank Chimek is cool." After talking it over a little, they added my name, too—Frank and I were the only two white people on earth they thought deserved to be saved.

But of course I couldn't say this to those men in the car. I thought of all the times I'd wanted to convince someone of something—convince a girl that I was the guy for her, or a teacher that my excuse was really real, or some guys who wanted to beat me that I didn't deserve to be beaten.

The driver said something about taking us back to the tree.

A deep voice from the back seat called out, "What you going to do with 'em, blood, lynch 'em?" The whole group laughed hysterically. I couldn't help smiling, though it felt like the smile of a crazy man.

"Let's lynch them *and* that sorry-ass tree," another voice from the back said. "Hang 'em all three from the overpass."

The driver waited until the laughter died. "I don't like white boys stealing niggers' trees," he said, "no matter how sorry the trees is, or the boys. Y'all move over and make room for these boys."

There was movement inside the car. A door clicked open. I jerked as if the click had come from a knife or a gun, and I guess Frank must have moved too. "Wait! Wait!" someone screeched. It was the girl. She scrambled forward so that her wide face and thick, round arms leaned over the front seat. "Take off your hood," she said to Frank.

Frank looked up from the street with that distant expression people and dogs wear just before they get beaten. "Fool!" the girl said, slapping at someone in the back seat. "Don't be pulling on me. Take off your hood," she repeated.

Frank looked at the driver.

"Go on," he said.

Frank untied the string and pushed the hood back, and his blond braids unfolded and fell all around him.

"I knew it!" the girl crowed. "They told me white folks couldn't do their hair like that, but I knew y'all could, I knew it. Come here—let me see."

Frank didn't move. He just stood there with his braids lying in lines against his scalp, snaking down around his shoulders, practically glowing in the dark.

"Damn, boy," the driver said, "did you get dunked in a tub of bleach?"

"Maybe he's an albino," the girl said. "Maybe he's really black." She and the man sitting in the passenger seat started arguing.

"C'mon, woman, a white black man? Give me a break."

"I saw a black albino once, man, in my social studies book. It was a purely white black man."

"Girl, you're talkin' about an Oreo."

"I'm talkin' about an albino—don't you know what an albino is?"

"Why don't y'all stop talking stupid?" the driver said. "The man is obviously white."

"For real," the deep-voiced man agreed, "he's some kind of white freak."

"Naw," another man from the back said, "he just wants to be black."

"Is that it, man?" the driver said to Frank. "Do you wish you was black?" Everyone in the car looked at Frank.

Frank lifted his head, his blond braids tilting back, and looked at all the faces looking at him. "Right now I do," he said simply, his face serious but hardly afraid, a hint of pleasure at his joke showing around his mouth and in his eyes.

The men in the car laughed suddenly, with surprise. "Right now I do," one of them repeated, and everyone laughed harder, with the deep-voiced man saying "No shit! No shit!" over and over between the laughter of the others.

When the laughter finally stopped, there was a floating sort of pause, like when you're standing on a teeter-totter with both ends off the ground. The driver said something to the others that I didn't quite hear—"Let's go" or "Let them go." Then he turned back to Frank. "I don't know why in hell you want that tree, man," he said, "but if you still want it, go on and take it—then take your crazy asses back home to Highland Park or wherever it is you're from before you run into some mean niggers or the police. And next time you want to steal a tree, go on out to Grosse

Pointe or Bloomfield Hills and steal yourself a nice *white* tree, something like a *pine* tree, all right?"

"All right," Frank said.

The driver shook his head. The car rumbled off. Frank and I walked, fast, back to the freeway slope and lifted the tree of heaven into the garbage bag. Then we walked down the slanting ground holding the bagged tree between us, checking the wide, gray freeway for cars.

The huge overpasses on either side were suspended at our level. We were leaning back against the pull of the slope, taking big strides. It felt like we were traveling between planets, like we were walking down from the sky. It felt like we were aliens— aliens in both worlds. But at least the world we were heading toward was home.

The
Angel
Thomas

For Stuart Dybek

Women haven't touched him since he died, and he hasn't eaten, and he hasn't felt the sun's warmth. Worst of all, he's been assigned a client who is severely depressed.

Thomas's client is still in her pajamas though it's one P.M. She is sitting at the kitchen table in her second-story flat stuffing Rice Chex into her face. Thomas is floating behind her chair. You could have made an omelet, Thomas thinks. And how about orange juice every now and then instead of always that bloody tomato? No wonder you keep thinking about killing yourself.

The woman stands and dumps the juice into the sink. Now look what you did, Thomas says silently. The woman looks down at her pajama top, grabs up a sponge, and scrubs at the tiny spots. The tomato juice smears into a haze of pink. A very large brooch will cover that, Thomas says. The woman returns to the table and lowers her face onto her arms. You're going to cry over stained pajamas? Thomas asks. Jesus Christ, why don't you just get it over with? Jump out the window or something.

I didn't mean it! Thomas thinks as the woman stands. The woman walks to the window anyway and opens it. A breeze blows in from the street, fluttering the curtains. In his last life Thomas's mother said God was everywhere, but Thomas can't help feeling that God can hear him better with the window open. Don't jump! he thinks. Life is worth it. Why don't you try to get out today, go to the beach, maybe—no, too cold for the beach—how about the park? Oh no, wrong thought, her boyfriend had ditched her in the park last week. The woman is leaning out the window, shoulders over the sidewalk—there's no front yard.

No wonder the woman's depressed, Thomas thinks. She's living above Six Mile, a commercial street, in the most murderous city in the nation. Second-most murderous, Thomas corrects himself: Detroit has recently dropped behind Atlanta. If the woman kills herself, Thomas wonders, will that boost Detroit's stats? That was an idle thought! he screams silently as the woman eases a knee onto the ledge. Listen, this whole idea is crazy—it's only two stories. You'll break a leg and they'll put you in a mental hospital. You think life is rough now . . .

The woman pulls her leg back into the room. Thomas leaves before he can mess things up worse. Floating over Palmer Park, he swoops down low, slips through the pond's surface, and swims down into the hazy green water. From the bottom he stares up at the water's skin. He had used to do this two lives ago, when he was Eva, a girl growing up in Bloomfield Hills. Eva would dive to the bottom of her parents' pool and turn over onto her back to escape her mother's plans for her: debate club, voice lessons, social dancing with midgets. Eva could lie underwater for only a few minutes. Thomas can lie like this for hours. He loves to watch the water's surface from underneath it. And submerged he feels removed from God.

He has to get hold of himself. What if his client had jumped? He had better watch out. His superior says God isn't punitive, but Thomas was sent back into life last time as a New Yorker with faulty balance and not enough height to reach subway straps, and that was right after Thomas caused the death of that flutist.

I wonder what he's doing now? Thomas thinks, settling into a pocket of the pond. In the past Thomas has been afraid that the flutist would come back to kill him in return. But the flutist has not seen Thomas alive since that morning their paths first crossed, during the last moments of Eva's life, at a Detroit Institute of Arts courtyard concert billed as "Brunch with Bach."

Eva thought the concert should have been called "Snack with a Stranger." The only food offered was fruit, coffee, and bread, and scanning the program she'd seen that the flutist, someone she'd not heard of, was to play his own compositions. Uncomfortably seated on a too-small scrolled iron chair, Eva's skepticism grew as the flutist walked into the courtyard. He was wearing baggy, tan, cotton pants and a shirt of off-white India cotton, with small singing birds embroidered around the yoke. His hair was as disarranged as a mystic's, he carried his flute as if it were a prize he disdained, and his face had the haughty, self-pleased look most people lose by the time they're twenty. Eva had resigned herself to a wasted morning.

She was paying closer attention to her indigestion than she was to the music when the music began to draw her in. Eva began thinking of her parents' pool. She hadn't lain on its floor in over forty years, and yet suddenly she was remembering the still water surrounding her, the flashing and sliding of the surface far above. The flutist was playing a melody that kept straying from its prettiness. The notes would stray confidently at first, as if they moved toward a desirable, mysterious goal. But the farther the notes strayed the less pretty they became; just short of becoming harsh, they would retreat step by step back into the melody. Hearing the music at its prettiest, Eva remembered the near harshness of the moments before. This both pleased and irritated her. It irked her that someone who didn't know her could bring back the layered water of her childhood.

The flute's song had once again grown almost harsh when stabbing pains struck Eva's chest. Before she could catch her breath, she had left her body and become Thomas. Disoriented and dazed, Thomas floated a few yards above the flutist's head. Half the concert-goers were gasping. A dozen of them had leapt up and were bending over Eva's prostrate shell. The flutist still played, but Thomas could hardly hear him. Thomas was floating higher, and the higher he floated, the fainter the music grew. Midnote he rose through the courtyard's mildewed cloth roof.

During that death Thomas was a supervisor. He wasn't supposed to have contact with the living. But Thomas wanted to hear the rest of the song, and so he floated down to earth.

He found the flutist taking a shower, daydreaming in the spray and steam. Silently, Thomas made his request.

"Come to my concerts if you want to hear me," the flutist answered.

Thomas went to three with no luck. He sought out the flutist again.

"Oh, that piece," the flutist said. "I've abandoned it. It was too harsh. The ending was weak, anyway, inconclusive. You wouldn't have liked it."

I want to hear it, Thomas said.

"I don't play it anymore."

Would you play it for me privately? Thomas asked.

"I don't give private recitals," the flutist said and turned the shower off.

That Sunday as the flutist was driving to his mother's, Thomas slipped into the car. Put aside the music itself, he said. Think of the interruption, of how you'd feel, for instance, if you had to leave your mother's table before dessert.

"I don't eat dessert," the flutist answered.

Think of this, then, Thomas said. You're in your car listening to a song on the radio, and you arrive at your destination before the song is over. You get out of your car anyway. Maybe you're not even thinking about the song, maybe you were hardly listening to it in the car, but a few minutes later you find yourself humming it: over and over and over, you can't get the tune out of your head. Now I didn't just step out of the car, I stepped—well, you can't even imagine the threshold I stepped over.

"I've had two near-death experiences," the flutist said.

Near-death! Near-death is like eating banana cake hot from the oven, death is—

"I preselect the music I wish to hear and record it. I don't listen to the radio."

Thomas stopped thinking to listen. He heard the squawking and tooting of woodwinds, like the chatter of deep-voiced birds. How would you like to get cut off from this? Thomas asked.

The flutist looked at his watch. "It won't happen. I won't arrive at my mother's for another fifteen minutes."

Your watch is wrong, Thomas said.

The flutist looked at his watch again.

Yi! Pull to the left quick! Thomas told him, and the flutist pulled in front of an accelerating semi.

Thomas focuses on the pond's surface again, noticing for the first time its film of tiny green seeds. I don't want to live again, he thinks. He'd come back into life after the flutist's death as Shorty, a big-footed, clumsy, subway-riding New Yorker shot to death at twenty-five for stumbling onto a stranger's foot. Shorty's life had been a wasteland except for Saturday night softball games. Eva'd been unhappy except when watching water from inside it.

A duck paddles over Thomas. What wonderful feet. Maybe they'll let me be a duck next time, Thomas thinks. If I could be anything I wanted to be, I'd be Judy Hamood's boyfriend. Judy Hamood! He hasn't thought of Judy since the last time he was twelve. He feels an erection coming on, but it's a flimsy thing, erection of the spirit.

And then he is out of the pond and being shaken as if he were a dog shaking water from itself. How can this be? Thomas thinks. I don't have a body.

I'll put you into a body, his superior answers, just so you can feel—

I want some answers, Thomas says. Every time I'm alive I think I'll find out the meaning of life *after* I die, then I die and remember being alive, but I never get a handle on what death is. Then I get born and forget I was ever dead until I die again. What do I have to do to talk to God? How many layers of angels is he hiding behind?

The superior doesn't answer. The shaking continues. At first Thomas tries to accommodate himself to the jerky rhythm, but finally he wrenches free and swoops up into the sky. He is moving fast, faster than ever before. Why hadn't he done this sooner? Instead of hiding in water, a part of God's planet.

Up, up, up, he passes through layer after layer of clouds, white and puffy and fat but really as thin as water. Soon the last layer of clouds is below him, a lumpy, cottony field. The air is pale blue. It's lonelier up here, Thomas thinks.

He is wondering how black space will look once he's in it, what the stars will look like, how close he'll be able to get to them, when he is surrounded. At first he thinks a horde of angels has circled him—he feels them on every side, above and below, he's surrounded completely. Then he realizes that only one, larger angel encircles him.

God! Thomas thinks. Is it you?

The air vibrates with unspoken emotion, laughter or sigh, Thomas can't tell. Thomas aches as if he has a body, or at least a chest, a hollow one. He passes through the large angel and swoops on.

The air grows paler and emptier. Thomas thinks of the beauty of air on earth, how it moved trees and the surface of water, sent trash skittering along streets. He thinks of how good the sun's warmth felt on his skin. Then for some reason he thinks of how the flutist never ate dessert. I always ate dessert, Thomas thinks, and even when I was living in New York City I liked the feel of air in my lungs.

Suddenly Thomas is passing through darkness, he is blind, eyelids pressed to his skull. He is moving underwater through the darkest water he's ever known.

He bursts into the light, howls as light stabs his eyes and air like fire pricks his lungs. Hands are on him. Voices are speaking in a language he doesn't understand. Faces are smiling and crying and staring at him. Sunlight shining in a window is warming his skin. He howls some more. He doesn't know who he is, where he is, who these people are, or whether he is crying for sadness or for joy.

Burning

On the night the '67 riots began, my family had just come home from vacationing in northern Canada. As we slept, still lulled by the place we'd just left (a stately lodge and pine cabins, a deep, ice-cold, clear lake), enraged Detroiters were setting fire to the city. We found out about it the next morning, around eleven o'clock, from Mrs. Willis, our next-door neighbor, who was returning from church as my father stepped out on our porch to get the paper. The police had raided a blind pig on 12th Street, Mrs. Willis told my father, and had arrested everyone in it. They'd beaten up one man pretty badly—thrown him up against a wall and clubbed him in the face. A crowd had gathered in the street, and after the police left the crowd started breaking windows and setting fires.

That was all Mrs. Willis knew, my father said, standing in our living room, paging through the paper's first section. He looked through it twice, scanning the sheets carefully, then tossed it aside without reading it and turned on the radio.

I was sick with pneumonia, as yet undiagnosed, and all that day I dozed and slept on the couch, waking sometimes at the radio or the TV or the sound of my father's voice. "What is this, some kind of a blackout?" I heard him say once.

"Why don't you leave it for a while," my mother answered, "and wait for the news at six?"

"Because I want to find out what's happening now," my father said. He had the radio on again and was fiddling through all the stations.

Most DJs didn't mention the riot at all, and those that did spoke of it indirectly. On WJLB, the soul station, Martha Jean the Queen talked about God and praying for Detroit and cooling it and staying home, and a male DJ from another station announced a super discount day on 12th Street, prices slashed to nothing, all you could carry for free. "Might be another price to pay, though," he added. "Might be higher."

Finally my father hit a station with hard news. The police had cordoned off a twenty-four-square-block area, the announcer said, but the "area of devastation" was much larger. Whole blocks of stores were going up in flames. Three people had been killed — a looter, a bystander, and a sniper. The governor had declared a state of emergency in Detroit, in Hamtramck, the small city to the east of us, and in our city, Highland Park. Two thousand extra police had been called in from all over the state, along with three thousand National Guardsmen.

"Damn, damn, damn," my father said softly, and he remained crouched by the radio without changing the station, even when a commercial came on.

I woke on the couch not knowing where I was until I heard my father and my brothers and some of the kids from our block playing ball in our front yard. I lay listening to the hard *thunk* of the tennis ball hitting the stoop, the deeper, softer sound it made when it connected with the bat, the cries and shouts of my brothers and of the Jones boys from across the street, and my father's loud and, to me, comforting voice. "Good hit," he'd call, or "Good try," or "Watch what you're doing—keep your eye on the ball." With my eyes closed, I listened to the sound of feet running the baselines (leading to and from home, these were dirt paths where the lawn had been worn away), and when I drifted off to sleep again, I dreamed of my father and my brothers and of Darryl and Dennis Jones running baselines that had been set on fire.

I woke again when my father came in and asked me how I was feeling.

"Okay," I said. "Tired."

He sat down beside me, laid his hand on my forehead, and looked off into space. I held still without watching him, relishing the way all his energy paused in that moment of almost-stopped time before he made his pronouncement. "Well, you're cool," he finally said. He rubbed my forehead as if lost in thought. Then he asked me if I was hungry.

I concentrated on my belly and the abstract idea of food. "Not really," I said. In the area of my belly I felt only the slight cramping caused by my period, which I'd begun for the first time just a day ago, a couple of hours before we started home from our vacation.

My father rubbed my forehead some more and then my shoulder, his large eyes frowning. I'd started our vacation with a bad cold, and on our second night in Canada I'd grown sicker. My parents had moved me into their cabin, where I proceeded to sleep night and day for the rest of the week, except during mealtimes, when my father woke me and led me as if I were elderly or blind up and down the rolling boardwalks to the central lodge.

The lodge was run like a restaurant, with menus the size of two placemats hinged together, and all week long my father had sat beside me and helped me to order: he'd look over my shoulder and prompt me in a gentle but enthusiastic voice. "How about the chicken? Your brothers claim it's great. Or soup is very easy to eat. Or you can just have dessert if you want."

I'd order the chicken or some soup and once strawberry short-cake but each time only take a bite or two. "I'm not the least bit hungry," I'd apologize, setting down my spoon or fork.

"That's all right," my father would assure me. "Don't eat it if you don't want it. You'll get your appetite back once you're feeling better."

I had never felt so tired and weak, but I wasn't worried at all. My father was a doctor, and, apart from this, I took for granted that he would keep me safe from any sort of harm. On the trip up to Canada, someone had cut off the car in the lane next to us, and the driver of the clipped car had slammed into the back of our station wagon, forcing us off the highway. My father had shouted, "Hang on!" and, grappling with the steering wheel as the wagon bounced along the weedy roadside, he had wrestled the car to a stop. No one was hurt, and nothing was damaged except for the wagon's back right corner, which was completely staved in. I had been lying with my head in that corner just a few minutes before we were hit but had moved to escape the shoes poking me from inside a duffel bag that my father had packed.

Now, as my father sat beside me on the couch, gathering wisps of hair from the edges of my face and smoothing them back against my head, I said, "Dad? What's going to happen?"

"You're going to start feeling better soon," he said. "Your mother is going to take you to the doctor tomorrow. You're looking a little better already—your eyes have lost that glazed look."

"I'm feeling a little better," I said. "I mean with the riot."

"Oh," my father said, and he pulled in his breath and let it out loudly and looked across the room while he thought of how to answer me. "It'll be over with in a little while, too," he said. "But it'll do more damage than your illness." He breathed in and out again, deeply and a little unsteadily, as if he needed more air in his lungs than he could get just by taking breaths. "I don't know exactly what will happen, honey," he said. "But you don't have to worry about it. Nothing will happen to you."

At supper that evening my appetite returned, and I ate more during that meal than I'd eaten all week. Afterward my whole family watched the news in the living room, gathered around the set: my little brothers, Danny and Zachary, sat to one side of me on the couch; my oldest brother, Michael, sat on the couch's far end; Arthur, who was twelve, a year older than me, knelt by the couch arm closest to the TV, my mother pulled up behind him in a dining room chair; and my father stood in front of us, to one side of the set, his gaze never leaving the screen.

The national newscaster talked about B-52 raids and firebombs exploding in a Saigon hotel, and the local newscaster talked about firebombs and fires and looting and sniping in Detroit. Rioting had broken out in other parts of the city, he said. Five more people had been killed during the day, and several hundred had been wounded. The area where the riot originated had spread to encompass 140 square blocks, south to downtown and north to Chicago Boulevard, with isolated fingers reaching out in all directions.

"Where's Chicago Boulevard?" Danny asked in his shrill little voice.

My father sighed and turned to look at him. "Do you know where Metro Hospital is?"

Danny nodded. Detroit Metropolitan was the hospital we went to when we needed to see a doctor and where our father worked as chief of psychiatry.

"Chicago Boulevard is about ten blocks south of Metro Hospital," my father said.

Michael and Arthur glanced at each other along the length of the couch.

"Are they going to burn the hospital?" Danny asked.

"No," my father said. "The hospital helps people. Now be quiet and let me hear this."

He began to pace, trying not to block anyone's view of the set, addressing the police commissioner when he came on the screen as if the man could hear him. "What did you think would happen," my father asked, "when you sent policemen who act like Klansmen into one of the poorest slums of the city, at a time when black people are so frustrated and angry that they're rioting all over the country?" When the newscaster said that Governor

Romney had given the police and guardsmen full authority to protect life and property, my father said, "In other words, he gave the go-ahead to shoot." He turned away from the set and paced and cursed a stream of curses.

I had watched my father rail all my life, against politicians on TV and whatever else displeased him. But that evening I watched more closely than I had before. This was our city on the news, not hundreds or thousands of miles away, but close enough for me to ride my bike to.

The following morning, my mother ushered me into our station wagon, backed out of our driveway, and headed west up McLean, gliding under the huge elms that formed an archway over our street and cast the big, old houses and front yards in deep shade. My father had left for the hospital a couple of hours before us—he had an eight o'clock patient, but my appointment wasn't until ten.

We crossed John R. and then Woodward, the main street of Highland Park as well as Detroit, and, jogging a little to our left, turned right onto Glendale. The houses outside my car window were as large as the ones on McLean, but on the other side of the street apartment buildings crowded the sidewalk—their front yards were small, and the buildings themselves looked a little run-down. So far we hadn't seen any people outside, and almost no cars. I thought of what Martha Jean, the soul station DJ, had said: that everybody should stay home.

The whole next block of Glendale on my mother's side of the car was taken up by Highland Park Junior College and Highland Park High, where Michael would begin when summer was over. Across the street from the high school and college were more slightly run-down apartments and two-family flats. Ahead of us, one block farther west, I could see the open, treeless space of Hamilton Avenue.

Hamilton was, like Woodward, a four-lane street, but Hamilton wasn't nearly as long as Woodward, and, unlike the section of Woodward that ran through our neighborhood, Hamilton was shabby and poor. I'd only seen it in passing, through the windows of our car, except for once last summer when my father and I had joined in a local march.

The march had come about after Highland Park police killed a ten-year-old boy while trying to shoot a fleeing burglary suspect. On the Saturday following the boy's death, about thirty Highland Parkers had marched in protest. We started on the street where the boy had lived and died and ended up at the police station, where we marched in a circle and then up onto the station steps. One man shouted that the police wouldn't shoot like that if it was their own child out on the street. Some of the marchers started crying and tapping on the station windows with their signs. Three policemen were sitting inside at desks. They didn't look out at us.

I assumed that if the police stood up and came outside, my father's presence would keep all of us safe. He was the only white adult in the march and the only man wearing a suit and a tie, and, on top of this, an expansive power emanated from him. This power shone from my father in all places, at all times, whether he was agitated or calm; it showed in the way that he held and carried himself, and in the tone of his voice and in the set of his face, and made people treat him as he expected them to. Five years before the Highland Park march, he had marched from Selma to Montgomery, after the first attempt, in which he hadn't participated, was broken up, bloodily, by police. After the first attempt, King had appeared on TV and asked for doctors to join in a second attempt in case they were needed to treat the wounded, and my father had driven down to Alabama and walked the whole route. During the second march, the police had not harmed a single marcher; all my father had had to do was wrap a sprained ankle.

I knew that my father wasn't solely responsible for keeping those policemen at bay. Yet I couldn't imagine anyone laying a hand on my father or daring to harm anyone who stood near him.

At the Highland Park march, the police remained at their desks the whole time that we stood on the station steps. We walked back down the steps and marched in front of the station some more, and then, finally, we left.

Now, as my mother and I glided across Hamilton in our station wagon, I turned around and tried to see the dead boy's church, which we had marched past. From my vantage point I couldn't recognize the storefront it had occupied. All the storefronts within my sight looked run-down and dirty. One had its windows boarded over. The sun beat down whitely along the length of the street, and broken glass gleamed from the sidewalks. I faced forward, shrinking toward the middle of the car seat, and stopped looking out. A couple of minutes later we reached the back of Metropolitan Hospital and parked in the lot behind the hospital's huge gray shape.

As I stepped from the cool car into the heat of the parking lot, I forgot all about my plan: to look for signs of the riot, happening just ten blocks south of the hospital, on the hospital's other side; as I slid across the seat and stepped into the sticky air, I felt my legs rub against the sanitary napkin between them, and all at once it struck me that this new condition of mine would be revealed if my doctor asked me, as he likely would, to take off all my clothes.

When I'd started menstruating two days ago it had caught me by surprise—my breasts had begun to develop, but I was only eleven, and, unlike many of the girls in my class, I hadn't been looking forward to or expecting this change yet. I'd mistaken the first few drops of blood for another symptom of my illness until my father explained to me what was happening. Oh yeah, we saw a movie about that at school last year, I'd thought, too sick and listless to care. My mother had bought me a box of sanitary napkins, and I'd held as still as a dog submitting to a collar while she showed me how to hook one to the belt. But now that I was beginning to feel better, I wasn't sure I wanted to be menstruating, and I certainly didn't want my doctor to see the awkward-looking pad and belt arrangement and my very private blood. I wanted to turn around and run back to the car and go home. Without thinking about it, my walking slowed almost to a stop. "Are you all right, honey?" my mother asked.

"No," I said, "I feel awful—I want to go home."

"Well, you have to see the doctor first, sweetie," my mother said. "Lean on me if you have to." And she put her arm around my shoulders and guided me forward.

The hospital halls were mostly empty, and the few patients I saw didn't look wounded, though my father had speculated that many victims of the riot would be brought here. Either the riot victims were coming in through the emergency entrance, I thought, or else the people I saw in the halls had wounds hidden under their clothing.

In the examination room, Doctor Chen asked me to remove my T-shirt but didn't say anything about taking off my jeans. After listening to my chest with a stethoscope, he told my mother I had pneumonia. The two of them discussed the progression of my illness and decided that I was over the worst of it. But I still needed lots of rest, Doctor Chen said, and also a penicillin shot.

The two other times I'd had penicillin shots, Doctor Chen had given them to me in the butt; then I had hated the shots because they hurt, but now the pain seemed insignificant compared to the prospect of removing my pants. "I don't want a penicillin shot," I said.

"No one ever does," Doctor Chen answered cheerfully. He went out into the hall; while we waited for him to return, I pleaded with my mother to stop him.

"Honey, please," my mother said. "Why are you making such a big deal out of this?"

I didn't tell her.

Doctor Chen came back with the needle and stood in front of me. "Okay, Annie," he said, "slip your pants down." I had pulled on my T-shirt while he was gone, and now I folded my arms across my chest and frowned at him. He looked me up and down as if I'd turned into some kind of rare bird. He'd been my doctor since I was three years old and had given me shots many times without me giving him any trouble. As he looked at me quizzically, something seemed to register in his eyes. "Would you rather take it in the arm?" he asked.

"I can take it in the arm?"

"You certainly can. Though it'll hurt less if you take it in the buttocks."

"I'll take it in the arm," I said.

He swabbed the flesh below my shoulder, inserted the needle, and slowly drove it in. I pursed my lips and squinted my eyes against the pain. "Antonia's getting to be a big girl," Doctor Chen said, withdrawing the needle. "Almost a young lady."

My mother smoothed her hand against the small of my back. I wanted to move away from her touch. I didn't usually notice the ways she chose to caress me, but suddenly her hand felt out of place.

As my mother and I left the hospital, again through the rear, I looked up at the sky. It was gray and hazy, and the air smelled bitter and sharp. "Is that smoke?" I asked, turning around and trying to see beyond the huge shape of the hospital to the riot and its fires.

"Yes it is, honey," my mother said sadly.

I wanted to stay and look at the sky and peer around the side of the hospital and see what was happening out in front, but at the same time I was relieved that my mother kept walking toward our car.

On the ride home, I slunk down on the seat. The struggle with my doctor had made me tired, my arm was sore from the shot, and there was that other, new pain that tugged at the center of my body. Yet my mind was clear. Now that I was beginning to get well, I felt like I was coming out of a daze; I felt as if I'd slept through much more than just a week of my life, and as if while I was away—far off in Canada and far off in my illness—everything had drastically changed.

That night at dinner my father said he'd seen the fires and some looters from his office window. He said he saw a man walking down the street holding what looked at first like a small pillow but turned out to be a whole ham. "And he was a white man, too," my father said. "This isn't about race. It's about being poor and being treated like shit."

We watched the news again that night after dinner. Seventy-five Americans had been killed in Vietnam, and thirty-six had been killed in Detroit. Toward the end of the newscast, President Johnson came on with a special announcement: he was sending the army to Detroit to quell the riot. Lawlessness and aggression could not be tolerated, he said, and would not be tolerated, abroad or at home. "Whose home are you talking about?" my father asked.

The set showed a clip of Johnson's face, his lips silently moving.

"Whatever happened to your war on poverty?" my father asked. "I guess you meant a war on poor people, you lying son of a bitch."

"Don't be so hard on him, Ralph," my mother said. "There aren't any easy answers."

"I'll give you an easy answer," my father said. "Give people jobs and treat them with dignity and respect."

"That's a good long-range answer," my mother said. "But right now things are totally out of control. This rioting isn't doing anyone any good—it's not doing the rioters any good, either."

"Don't you think I know that," my father said.

The following day, four thousand federal troups arrived in Detroit. They came in planes and brought copters and tanks. We saw the tanks rolling up Grand River Avenue on the morning news. My father didn't say anything, except for a soft stream of curses when he burned his mouth on his coffee. The air conditioner was on, and he had just showered, but he was already sweating.

Shortly after my father left for work, Danny came into the house shrieking. "The police are going to shoot! The police have big guns, and they're getting ready to shoot!"

"No, they're not," my mother said in an unconvincing voice. She and Danny and I moved to the front windows, staying back from them a couple of feet, and looked out through the gauzy blue curtains. A Highland Park patrol car was creeping up our street as slowly as a tank with two huge, high-powered rifles propped outside the windows of the car: each policeman, driver and passenger, rested his forearm outside his window, with his hand curved around a rifle butt and the rifle barrel slanted at the sky.

"I was going over to Kelvin's house," Danny said, "and then I looked up, and they were coming to shoot me."

"No they weren't, they wouldn't do that," my mother said, stroking Danny's neck as we watched the car creep past our front yard. But she told all of us, even my two older brothers, to stay in the house or our backyard.

I thought of the ten-year-old boy that the Highland Park police had shot the previous summer. I hadn't thought about him much at the time. I didn't know that he'd existed until after he was dead—he hadn't gone to my school, and I never saw the street he'd lived on until we marched there. The tragedy of the boy's death only hit me when I saw two women marchers—the boy's mother and his aunt, I guessed—weeping on the police station steps. Even then I couldn't imagine their anguish completely, and, after the march ended, the boy and his death had drifted from my thoughts.

But seeing the police flaunting their big guns on my own block brought the boy's death back to me and filled me with immediate dread. I didn't think that the police would shoot me or my brothers—they wouldn't shoot white children, I knew, or almost knew. But they might shoot one of our friends, or one of the kids from our school.

The patrol cars with guns thrust outside their windows crept by our house all day long. I watched them from the curtains twice, then retreated to the couch and stayed there, wishing our curtains were heavier, harder to see through. I was still menstruating, and each time I felt a cramp or went to the bathroom and saw the blood, I thought of gunshot wounds and other violence, though my mother had explained to me that the cramping and the blood leaving my body were natural functions and a sign of health.

That evening when my father came home from work my mother told him about the policemen and their guns. "Those stupid sons of bitches," my father said, shaking his head bitterly, and instead of going upstairs as he usually did to change out of his suit, he stayed in the living room. "Do you know," he said to my mother, "that it's illegal for our whole family to walk down our own street, even in the daytime?"

She looked at him sadly and a little blankly, the same look she'd had on her face all day.

"No more than three people are allowed to walk or gather together on a public street anywhere in the city," my father said. He paced up and down the living room. "This is like a police state. Our so-called democracy. Do you know that Romney told the Guard to shoot looters even if they're running away? Most of the people who have been killed so far have been looters shot in the back, including a couple of teenagers." He picked up *The Fishes*, one of the Time-Life nature books he had bought for us kids, and sat down on the blue swivel chair near the living room windows. I watched him flip through the book's pages. I could tell he wasn't really reading but was doing what I did: looking at the pictures, skimming the lengthy captions.

The police cruised by our house about fifteen minutes later, shortly before we were to eat. My mother was in the kitchen, my brothers were scattered upstairs and in the backyard. I was looking at another book from the Time-Life set, propped up on cushions on the couch. My father had put down his book and stood up and was taking off the jacket of his suit. He was standing with his back to the living room windows, and I don't know if the police cars or their rifles glinted or if my father simply sensed them, but he turned as they came up the street and moved to the windows to watch them.

He stood where the air conditioner parted the curtains, his tie blowing askew and his face angry and tense. "Look at those bastards parading their power," he said. "Scared, stupid sons of bitches." He was about to say something else, to comment or curse, when I saw his face change at something new that he was seeing. I sat up straight and looked out through the filmy curtains. The police car had stopped next door to our house, and the two policemen in it were talking to one of our neighbors.

"Annie, who is that? Do you know?" my father asked, jerking his head toward the street.

I got up and joined my father at the window, resting my fingers on the sill. I was standing only inches from the glass, but I felt safe with my father right beside me. "I think it's David Jenkins," I said. "Yeah, it's him."

"Do you know him?" my father asked.

"Sort of. He's in Michael's class. He lives down at the end of our street."

Abruptly, my father left his place at the window and went out the front door. The screen door slammed, and I started after him; by the time I reached the edge of our porch, my father was out in the street. I stayed on the porch, halfway hidden behind a pillar, resting my hands against the rough bricks. The dirt baseline from home to first ran in a straight line from me to my father and David and the patrol car with the policemen in it.

"This young man lives here," my father said to the policemen sitting in their car. "He's thirteen or fourteen years old, and he lives on this street."

The police said something I didn't hear. Huge black sunglasses hid their eyes, and their lips looked as pale as their skin. Their rifles, thrust outside their windows, still rested on their forearms, angled toward the sky.

"He's half a block from his house," my father said. "He was just walking down his own street in broad daylight."

The police spoke again, still too softly for me to hear, and again my father answered them: "*You're* the ones who need to be checked—what do you think you're doing, riding around with your guns hanging out all over the place? You're just looking for trouble—you're going to start trouble."

My father was standing three feet from the policemen and their rifles, but he didn't seem the least bit frightened. Maybe he was too angry to be afraid, or maybe he assumed, as I did, that the police wouldn't shoot at him no matter what he said to them.

While my father and the police spoke, David stood very still, not saying a word or even opening his lips, his dark face turned partly away from my father and the policemen and me; he was looking up the street toward Woodward, looking at nothing in particular, or at something I couldn't see.

"The curfew doesn't start until dusk," my father said. "Three more hours, at least. You have no reason to stop him."

David was still staring up toward Woodward, without moving a muscle of his body or face. But then, unseen by my father, David's face shifted toward us, and his eyes burned at my father with hatred.

I felt my cheeks flush and grow hot, and I glanced down at the stoop, my hands gripping the edges of the pillar's rough bricks. I wanted to disappear without effort and find myself returned to the living room couch. But I also didn't want to leave. I looked along the baseline to David and my father and the policemen with their guns and imagined running to them along the bare line of earth. Maybe that would be enough to break things up, and I'd stop when I reached the edge of their group. Or maybe I'd keep running toward them and burst like a fireball into their midst. But even as I thought of it, I knew I wouldn't do either of these things or anything else; I knew that I was wholly powerless to change things for the better. And besides, I was suddenly afraid, even with my father to protect me.

"I don't care if there's been looting on Hamilton," my father said. "There's been no looting, no trouble of any kind, in this neighborhood. And by riding around like this, flaunting your muscle, you're just making everything worse."

The policeman next to the curb got out of the car, holding his rifle close to his chest. He spoke to David, and David spread his legs and placed his hands on the car's hood. Then the policeman slid the barrel of his rifle up and down the insides of David's legs. My father looked between the two policemen, the one standing behind David and the one still in the car, and said something I didn't hear. Years later he told me that he'd said something like "Come on now, that's enough."

At my father's words, the policeman standing behind David lifted his chin up and laughed. Then he leveled his gun until it was pointed at David; from where I stood, it seemed to be resting on David's back. My father turned slowly to the policeman still sitting in the car, and a note came into his voice that I'd never heard there before, a note that made me think of my own voice when I was about to cry. "Will you talk to your partner?" he asked. "Will you please talk to your partner?"

I had never seen or heard my father come anywhere close to tears. Years later, I saw him weep many times—once, when Michael reached draft age, at the prospect of his going to Canada or to jail; and again and again, when Danny was nineteen, after his legs were severed at a summer factory job; and, a few weeks after Danny's legs were amputated, at the death of my newborn child. But when I stood watching my father plead with and exhort the policemen, these things were far in the future, and my father was to me, or until that moment he had been, invincible, incapable of losing.

My father continued to talk with the police. David remained with his hands on the car hood, the gun still pointed at him. I drew all the way back behind the pillar and leaned against the roughness of the bricks. I should go into the house, I knew, and, when my father came in, act as if I hadn't followed him out. And that's what I did. But first I stayed hidden behind the pillar a little longer, my arms and hands wedged between my body and the bricks, feeling, from deep inside me, the pull of my blood leaving and listening to the faltering sound of my father's voice.

Self-Defense

I put up with the red-haired girl until the day she cut me off doing laps in lifesaving class; then I grabbed onto her leg, climbed onto her back, and pushed her red head under water. Unfortunately, I went under, too. The karate lessons I'd been taking did me no good as we struggled, but for once the six-foot beauty was my height. I considered the prospect of her head never rising higher than mine again. Keep her down, keep her down, I thought.

After she escaped, I sat on the edge of the pool and stared at my feet and at nothing, feeling relaxed and unburdened and dazed, until the teacher laid her hand on my shoulder. I flinched away from her, my heart leaping. My fellow students, ringing the pool like white seals, were glancing at me as if I were a visitor from the Twilight Zone. "Go to your counselor, Annie," the teacher said, pointing at the green tiles leading to the locker room. "Now. Bring me a pink slip tomorrow."

While I dressed I imagined how much worse things could be: I could be a landless Brazilian tenant farmer, living in a shack of tin and cardboard; I could be a political prisoner, tortured daily in Argentina. Or, a vision more heart-stopping because I could imagine it more clearly, I could find myself back in my old neighborhood and walking in Nigger Park, so named by the black kids because whites weren't allowed there.

Stepping from the locker room into the empty hall of Redford High, I felt a sudden, strange longing for that place I'd left behind—not Nigger Park, but Highland Park, where I'd lived most of my life. We had moved from there right after I finished tenth grade, four months after I was attacked outside the high school by a group of forty black girls I didn't know. Highland Park High was ninety-nine percent black by then, and I was one of three white students left there who weren't poor.

At my new school, somewhere among my thousands of white, middle-class peers, I would fit in, I had thought. But after eight months of floating from group to group, I'd begun to realize that, despite my being of the majority color and class, I might not fit in at Redford either. To make things worse, the red-haired girl and her three big boyfriends wrestled in the hall during every class break, knocking into anyone who was in their way, and since my locker was right next to theirs, they always came slamming into me. I'd try to keep my balance and get my lock open before they messed the numbers up. Or I'd get out of their way, fuming, and wait to get my books until after the late bell rang. I had taken for granted that at my new school I would not be harassed in any way, and, no matter how I tried to prepare myself, it scared me when in the midst of twirling my lock I was suddenly jolted and sent flying. For a second I would think I was back at my old school and truly being attacked; my shoulder or back or wherever I was struck bothered me less than the wild beating of my heart.

My counselor was eating a meatball sandwich when I walked into her faded office. Such food seemed much too robust for her—she was a quiet, poised, wrinkled woman—but she was eating the sandwich with a knife and fork and chewing with her mouth delicately closed. Mrs. Rubin swallowed her small mouthful of food and pushed her sandwich in its nest of foil aside. "Is it raining?" she asked, glancing to the side of my head and back to my face.

"No," I said, "I was swimming. In lifesaving class. My teacher sent me."

"Why don't you have a seat," Mrs. Rubin said.

She was sitting on a straight wooden chair pulled up to an ancient oak desk. Behind her, elegant windows rose almost to the ceiling. I sat down on another straight wooden chair and tried to look like a responsible student.

"Why don't you tell me why you're here," Mrs. Rubin said.

I looked into her pale blue eyes. "I pushed a girl's head underwater and tried to hold it there," I said.

"What precipitated this?" Mrs. Rubin asked, staring at me glassily, as if bored.

"You mean in the beginning?" I asked. "Or today?"

"Let's start with today," Mrs. Rubin said, and I saw a glittering coming from deep inside her eyes. Suddenly I liked her pretty well. In fact, I realized I'd liked her all along, from the moment I'd first seen the lizardy wrinkles of her throat. Once when I was complaining about a teacher to Wild John, my Highland Park counselor, he said that I always did one of two things with people: I either took them into my lap or I threw them against the wall. I wondered what Wild John would tell me now.

Mrs. Rubin cleared her throat so delicately it sounded like humming. I paused before answering, trying to steady my breathing, thinking that someday when I mastered karate I'd be able to steady my heartbeat.

By the time I got out of my counselor's office, school was over. I considered stopping at my hall locker but could not rid myself of a disturbing picture: the red-haired girl's three hard-muscled, hard-eyed boyfriends leaning on the hall lockers to either side of mine. I flipped the picture out of my head as if out of a stack of Polaroids, not looking where it landed, and left the school, walking down Grand River, a street, not a river, a desert, really, six lanes wide and treeless, as hot and blowing and gritty as if it were already summer.

I walked holding the slip my counselor had signed, turning around every now and then to make sure no one was behind me. Nothing written on the slip even hinted at what I'd done; Mrs. Rubin had written the time, the date, her name, my name, and that was all. I could forge my mother's name to the slip, or I could confess to my mom that I was in trouble, as I really was, for being light years behind on my hooked rug for Home Ec. I would not tell my father anything, as I wasn't talking to him during those years unless I had to. I was angry at him—because he blasted opera from his Cobo Hall–size speakers every morning at six, when I didn't have to get up till seven; and because he denounced racism, poverty, and the war in Vietnam but spent too little of his money and time in ridding the world of these things; and because he had a mistress, a fact I'd deduced on my own but that I never thought about except for sometimes at night when I was struck by my mother's face, closed down over its pain, and realized that my father wasn't home.

By the time I got home from school I was sweaty and flecked with grit from the street. It was Thursday, my night to cook dinner. I washed my hands and arms, then opened cans of tomatoes for chili, thinking of R. T., my recently dismissed boyfriend. I had told R. T. good-bye two months ago, but I missed his white people jokes—they were simply black people jokes turned around—and I missed lying on my mother's couch with him while he sang Al Green songs: "You Ought to Be with Me" and "Let's Stay Together." R. T. had followed me home from Redford High one day, and I'd liked that, too—usually I chose my boyfriends, and it felt like being on vacation, to get a boyfriend without having to do any maneuvering.

But once R. T. had won me over to him he revealed some disquieting notions, such as that when white "girls" and black men were "keeping company" the white girl had to "look really good" or else black people would think the man was only interested in her because she was white. R. T. tried to talk me into not washing my hair (he liked how my hair, when dirty, lay flat against my head), and he tried to talk me into losing weight. He'd open his wallet to the picture of Wanda, a rail-thin yellow-hued girl he'd left behind in Alabama. "Don't you think you'd look good about this shape?" he'd say.

R. T. had also tried to talk me out of taking karate; he said that the black-and-blue marks covering my lower legs were too ugly and that I didn't need to know how to fight, that he would take care of me. In the two months since we'd parted company, my legs had stopped bruising—upon being struck, they swelled instead—and my body had grown leaner and harder. R. T. called me once and said he wanted to get back together. I told him no.

Now, though I still didn't want to get back with him, I imagined R. T. pitted against the red-haired girl's boyfriends—R. T., whose skinny legs I'd feared would snap when he played basketball with my brothers, R. T., who carried a phone, not a gun, in his car. He'd pretend at red lights that the phone actually worked and he was talking to someone. R. T. had the laugh of a loon. He was not a fighter, and even if he'd been a black belt and still my boyfriend, I would not have felt happy about having him for a protector. I didn't want to count on him or on anyone, because sometime or other I'd be sure to be caught alone. I'd been lucky on that day I was attacked at my old school—some of my classmates had stepped forward and saved me. I was grateful, but I wished that I'd been saved sooner—before what seemed like a hundred hands strained toward me, before those hands pulled my hair and tore my clothes, forced me into the street and onto my back and gouged the flesh around my eyes—and I wished even more that I had saved myself. I wondered if I would have been attacked at all if I had been an expert at karate. My karate teacher said that if you learned karate well enough, you didn't have to use it, that once you learned to defend yourself, you rarely needed to.

As I separated garlic from its skin, giving each clove a sharp whack with the butt of my big chef's knife, I thought of all the people I'd known in Highland Park who hadn't been able to defend themselves—neighbors, classmates, and friends who had been knifed, and hit with brass knuckles and bricks, and raped, and one who had been shot in the head and killed on his own front lawn.

———————

I was mincing the garlic, rocking the big knife up and down, when my brother Arthur came home from his job at the Grand River and Kentford McDonald's. "More meat—oh no," he said at the ground beef frying on the stove. "If only it weren't so greasy. If only it weren't so gray. If only it didn't invade my dreams and every minute of my waking life."

"I didn't forget you," I answered, touching the tip of the knife to the little pot of chili that I'd separated out from the big pot and set on a back burner.

"Oh good," Arthur said. He opened the refrigerator, took out a beer, and chugged half of it down. His straight, dark blond hair, pulled tightly back from his face, exaggerated his huge eyes and his large nose and mouth. Arthur was eighteen, a little more than a year older than me, but he'd graduated from high school at sixteen because the Catholic school where he had transferred to get away from his Highland Park druggie friends had found it easier to graduate him than to kick him out. Since then Arthur had worked in a diner in Indiana and a cafeteria in Ohio and camped in the Keys, living off fish he caught. Between times he'd come home for two and three weeks. He'd been home now for two months.

"Look what I got in school today," I said, pulling the pink slip out of my pocket.

Arthur took the slip from me, unfolded it, and read it aloud: "Two-twenty P.M., May 15, 1974, Antonia Zito, H. Rubin— What is it, a raffle ticket?"

"It's from my counselor for getting in trouble today."

"Oh yeah? What'd you do?"

"Tried to drown that red-haired girl."

Arthur got out another beer and palmed himself up onto the counter. "How close did you come to succeeding?" he asked.

"Not very. In fact, I almost drowned myself."

I told him about the red-haired girl running into me with her feet and me climbing onto her back and the two of us struggling underwater.

"So how did it end?" Arthur asked.

"She got away. By that time the two of us were practically dying. Then the teacher swam up and rescued the red-haired girl."

"She saved that harlot and left you to drown?"

"Well, I wasn't drowning as badly. I was only gasping. The red-haired girl was choking."

"The girl should have been shot," Arthur said.

I let out a cry of protest that sounded more like a cry of delight. But my pleasure faded as I started thinking again about the red-haired girl's boyfriends: about how they were all six feet or taller and looked like football players, about how I'd often seen their muscles as they wrestled with the red-haired girl. Even though they were just playing around, they made the lockers bang and rumble like thunder. Again I flipped the picture of them out of my mind. "What do you think I should do about this slip?" I asked Arthur. "I'm supposed to have a parent sign it and return it to my teacher tomorrow."

"Oh, they're not serious about these things," Arthur said, setting the slip on the counter a fraction of an inch from a pool of water. "It's their job to overinflate these little slips' importance and to pretend to feel that they've failed unless they transmit that gravity onto you. I'd either sign Mom's name to it and turn it in or throw it out."

"And not say anything to Mom?" I picked up the slip, folded it, and tucked it into my pocket.

"You'd only worry her."

"But she'd probably want to know."

"Nini, you're nearly an adult now. Are you going to bring all your little problems to her for the rest of your life?"

"It's easy for you to be so casual about it," I said. "You can just take off for Indiana or the Keys whenever you want."

"Actually, I'm thinking of going to California."

I turned back to the stove and pushed the meat from the frying pan into the big pot of tomatoes, regretting that I'd troubled to keep Arthur's chili separate. But I'd managed without Arthur, and I'd manage without him again. Pretty soon we'd both be grown up, and then he'd always be somewhere far off and I'd be lucky if I saw him once a year.

Just before I left Mrs. Rubin's office she'd said, "I wish I had advice for you, Antonia, but I think you know enough to figure things out for yourself." Figure out what things? I'd wanted to ask. I knew better than to try to drown the red-haired girl before I pushed her under. As for the bigger things, such as what I wanted to do for the whole rest of my life, all the time looming closer, no, I didn't know. And I wouldn't have anyone to talk to after Arthur left. Mike, my oldest brother, was away at college, my younger brothers were too young, and my parents were no help at all: when my mom didn't find life easy, she bore it, and my dad didn't expect life to be nice; its major flaw, according to him, was that "people are no damn good." When I was thirteen and fourteen and he would say this, I'd remind him that he was a person. He'd answer that he was an exception, he and a few of his friends.

I was able to avoid my parents at dinner that evening without raising suspicion, as I always went without dinner on the nights I attended karate. While my family ate, I sat on my bed and thought about staying home and working on my hooked rug, maybe even getting my mom and Arthur to work on it with me, as they had on a couple of occasions. Hooking along with Arthur on one side of me and our mom on the other, I might ease into the subject of my slip. Arthur was so good at making an argument—his tone, his words, his gestures would win our mom to his point of view. She wouldn't even have to unfold the little piece of paper, I wouldn't even have to take the thing out of my pocket. "Oh, that's okay, honey, just sign it yourself," she would say.

I buried the slip in my desk drawer that held the miscellaneous stuff I didn't know what else to do with, left the house by the back door, and drove up Grand River in the station wagon, our mom's car, a five-year-old luxury liner that occasionally stalled turning right for no reason mechanics could figure. I'd learned to kick the dashboard when this happened, not death-dealing karate blows, but hard slams with the bottom of my gym shoe to which the dashboard was impervious. This did not make the car start up again, but I felt better afterward for having expended such cruel force without clueing anyone to my behavior.

As I drove an idea came to me: maybe my mom would let me drop her off at work every day for the rest of the school year; then I could drive to Redford and use the car to store my books between classes. Redford High was huge, with over four thousand students. If I avoided the hallway where my locker was located, quit my lifesaving class, and kept a careful watch besides, chances were that I could avoid the red-haired girl and her boyfriends until they graduated. Since I was short, and Redford was mostly white, I could easily lose myself in the crowds.

But I doubted my mom would let me keep the car unless I gave her a good reason. My mom had never been in a fight, had never even got into trouble in school. It would be difficult to explain to her my trying to drown one of my classmates and wanting to use the station wagon as my hall locker.

I parked on Grand River a block from the gym. Nam, my karate teacher's eighteen-year-old son, was sitting outside the gym door in his street clothes, drinking a take-out Coke with a straw. Nam looked up as I walked in the door and flashed me his usual stiff but friendly smile. Good, I thought, he hadn't heard about what I'd tried to do.

Nam often trained at the gym, he occasionally taught his father's classes, and he was one of my locker partners at school, but I didn't know him very well—I was only his and his sisters' locker partner because, having begun karate lessons during the summer, I knew Nam, Chi, and Shim at the beginning of the school year better than anyone else at Redford. I'd never talked to Nam about the red-haired girl or about much of anything else. He didn't speak English well, and at school he was always in a hurry, head scrunched to the lock, winglike shoulders braced as if by magic against the red-haired girl and her admirers.

I skirted the gym, brushing the wall as I passed sparring green and red belts until I reached the women's dressing room, a tiny, curtained-off space the size of a walk-in closet. I was thinking of the locker boys again and wondering if Nam would at any point step in to save me. Surely at some point he would, but his idea of what that point should be might be different from mine. I'd heard a rumor that Suk, the second-to-youngest Park, had angered his father because he'd fought with classmates at his junior high. The story was that the other students had said, "Show us some karate, you little runt," and Suk Park, who looked like a furious whirl-wind when he worked out on the bag, had laid the three bigger boys on their backs. Only twelve years old, Suk was an upper-level red belt, ready to test for his black. But his father had banned him from the gym and delayed his examination time indefinitely. "Walk around trouble," Mr. Park had admonished the class more than once. "When to use MooDooKwanTang-SooDo is much important as how."

I changed into my uniform, removing my jeans and replacing them with white karate pants before taking off my outer shirt, pulling on my tunic, and tying my belt over my flat, hard belly. As a plump, slow-moving eleven year old, I'd dreamed of taking off to the woods and living on wild foods; I'd imagined myself losing weight and becoming graceful and swift. At one with my body and my surroundings, I would run like an Indian girl or even a deer. I had abandoned that dream long ago, but now, learning karate, my body had begun to achieve the grace, speed, and strength that I had imagined. It was only a matter of time, I thought, before my purple belt was replaced by a green belt, then a red, and finally a black. I'd been taking karate for the eleven months since we'd moved from Highland Park, attending classes two or three times a week, practicing kicks and punches and katas almost daily.

I parted the curtain, stepped out of the dressing room, and noticed that all the sparring had stopped. This was unusual—most evenings, the gym was a lively place in the minutes before class began. Five red belts were doing standing stretches, spread out along one wall, but all the other twenty or so men were sitting cross-legged on the two mats farthest from the front of the gym. Some were talking and listening to each other with a keyed-up, solemn interest; those that were silent gave off an air of gravity and disturbance. Mr. Park stood at the front of the gym, hands on hips, alternately talking with Nam and looking out over his seated, uneasy students.

I walked to an empty mat, sat down grasping my feet, and pressed my heels together. A wave of heat infused me—the atmosphere of the gym suddenly seemed like that of the pool room after I'd dragged myself out of the water to find the whole class trying not to stare at me. But my thought was ridiculous—these fellow students could not know what I'd tried to do; except for a new white belt, who had glanced at me without recognition when I'd first walked in, these students were all post–high school age, and even Nam, my own locker partner, hadn't heard about what I'd done. Mr. Park, Nam, the others—none of them knew.

I bowed my knees up and down like wings, a warm-up I'd come to perform without thought. Then, stopping bowing, I rolled my head—slowly, slowly, slowly, always slowly, Mr. Park had warned. Even he still rolled his head slowly, he said, the neck was so very delicate.

Mr. Park clapped his hands. We fell into lines unhurriedly, the more advanced students at the front, the white belt, me, and two leftover green belts ending up each of the four long rows. Mr. Park said, "Good evening," and we answered him. Some of the upper-level red belts inclined their heads. I was lost between two thoughts: deciding that I couldn't tell my mother about the red-haired girl because she would tell my father and he would break our silence with some psychologically insightful but snide remark, and also thinking about Herb Hills, the neighbor of ours in Highland Park who had been killed on his front lawn. I hadn't yet figured out a way to phrase the question, How do you prevent a bullet from reaching your head? I doubted very much that Mr. Park had an answer. I was lost in the murk that exists between uninspiring thoughts when Mr. Park snapped me alert. Instead of leading us in warm-ups, as he usually did, he was speaking.

"I have been hearing whispering," Mr. Park said. The room grew still, and it already had been still. The shushing of uniforms quieted as if a wind had ceased. "And I like to say, Yes, it is true that one of our students had an unfortunate thing . . ." He continued to speak—I could see his lips moving—but I couldn't hear him. How had he found out? From Nam? How much did Nam know? How much had he told? I imagined Mr. Park calling me to the front of the gym, saying something quiet and grave, then sending me to the dressing room; I imagined that street clothes were the only kind of clothes I would wear again.

But no one was thinking about me. I could hear Mr. Park's voice again; my heart flapping like a bird, I shifted so I could see him.

"If this student not panicked, he not been hurt. It is very fortunate that the thiefs were interested in his wallet only. He could been hurt very badly. This student very good student, has knowledge—fight well." Mr. Park opened his left hand and beat it lightly with his right fist. "Students," he said, "the mind must go with the body. We making fight simulation here, yes, but is not game, is not game. You will use what is learned here very well if keeping your head." I thought of my Highland Park neighbor again. No one knew if Herb had panicked. There had been no signs of struggle. I was torn between hoping he hadn't known what hit him and wanting him to have made an avoidable mistake, besides stepping outside in a neighborhood where violence was commonplace.

Mr. Park proceeded to lead us through warm-up, spending a long time on easy, single kicks and grapples—straightforward, unfancy defenses that untrained people might effectively use. Twice he stopped the class and made several red belts move through single front kicks to harder, but still basic, combinations: front-back, side-back, round-back. You could see that Mr. Park was disturbed about the student he hadn't named, yet his movements as he demonstrated what he wanted to see from us were as fluid and swift as on any other day. His karate pants floated and snapped, his body blurred like a hummingbird's wings, then clicked into focus. He made karate look natural, as graceful as dancing, but faster and stronger and more intense.

After basic instruction, Mr. Park led us through the first kata, a series of karate moves executed flowingly, slowly, without pause. As we moved, separately and together, the occasional screech of a bare foot on the wood came to me as if from a long distance, muffled as it was by my own slow breath. I understood my own body, that it began at my center and extended outward to the limits of my skin. And I knew so well by heart each next step I would take that my mind and body seemed to drift together, indistinguishable from one another.

After two more katas and runs at the bag, it was time for the part of class that I dreaded. Mr. Park pointed to ten of us, and we lined up facing our designated opponents. I didn't look my opponent, the big new white belt, in the face. I would have had to tilt my head back, and I didn't want him to see the defeat I was already feeling—even if I won against him, my legs would ache and swell, as they had every time I'd sparred this month.

I waited for Mr. Park's beginning signal, trying to calm myself, my heartbeats tripping into a blur. It felt as if my single heartbeats might become one long, drawn-out beat that was the same as no beat. I knew this wouldn't happen, I knew that I wouldn't die, but I was afraid I might get smashed by a misaimed elbow or foot or fist.

Mr. Park asked the ten of us to bow and then said, "Okay, fight." The white belt and I began to shift from foot to foot. His long arms swayed, reminding me of clubs. We sidled around each other, pretending to spar, throwing a kick and a punch here and there to make ourselves look good, but keeping our distance.

"C'mon, you purple belt, white belt, fight!" Mr. Park called. I saw that my opponent would not dig in first—though a head taller than me and a good thirty pounds heavier, he was afraid of me, of my colored belt. So without thinking further I faked a front kick with my left foot, then snapped a right side kick at his thigh and leaped at him, striking his right arm down and grabbing his uniform at the throat, bringing my left arm up as if to snap back his head.

"Nicely, very nicely," Mr. Park said, but I couldn't look to see if he was complimenting me or someone in one of the other fights heating up on all sides.

The white belt tried to imitate my rush, but I knocked his arm away, roughly, of necessity, since his approach had been overly forceful. We fought heatedly for another few minutes, each of us blocking the other successfully. My legs began to ache from all the blocks as they never had before—this white belt's arms were heavy and bony, and he blocked with clumsy force. Each block was a blow, which caused me to kick more and more slowly. My last kick was so slow that the white belt could have grabbed my foot if he'd tried. As he struck it down with his sharp wrist I noticed that my ankle looked very strangely shaped. "Wait a minute," I said. "Stop." He let his arms fall to his sides, and I backed away from him and bent over and lifted my pants legs. My calves and ankles had ballooned. They were inches fatter than usual. My ankle bones and my ankles themselves had disappeared beneath the swelled flesh.

"Don't stop fighting!" Mr. Park called. "There is no stopping in real fighting."

I walked over to him, feeling too awed by the sudden ballooning of my legs to answer.

"Go back, keep fighting," Mr. Park said.

I lifted my pants legs to show him.

He looked quickly and looked away. "Go sit down," he said quietly, his lips tight.

I sat on the mats and watched the other fighters, feeling defeated and startled and frightened, as well as awed. As I stared at my huge, numbed legs I grew dizzy. My legs had never swelled so quickly, or so horrendously, and I wasn't sure what the swelling meant. I'd always asked my father about my body, even when I began to menstruate, since, being a psychiatrist, he was also a medical doctor. He'd always had answers, clear and complete. But I'd stopped speaking to him, and I hadn't spoken to anyone else, either, about my legs. I'd hoped that, just as they had overcome their tendency to bruise, they would overcome their tendency to swell. Worrying about my legs, watching the fighters, I felt an invisible boundary spreading between us, a boundary that had always existed, but one that until now had grown narrower and that I had assumed would eventually disappear.

After class, changing in the women's dressing room, I could hear the men talking congenially on the other side, but not what they were saying. As I walked toward the front of the gym I looked for Nam, but he had already left. I stepped out onto the street. Grand River still looked like a desert, though it was beginning to grow dark. The pavement shone light gray with mica glitters as if the moon rather than street lights were lighting it up.

I had walked a few steps down Grand River when I heard Mr. Park in the doorway behind me. "You take a rest," he said. I turned and smiled at him gratefully, but after I'd turned around again and continued down the street I wondered if he'd meant I shouldn't come back to the gym until I could spar without stopping. Mr. Park did not allow students to come to class and not fight, and he also did not allow us to wear shin guards or padded clothing. He wanted to toughen us, he wanted us to be prepared.

I locked myself into the station wagon and drove and found myself at home without remembering how I got there. Through the front windows I could see my mom sewing, her head bent, her lips pursed, her hands, below the windows, moving out of my line of sight. I thought of going in the front door and telling her that Arthur was thinking of taking off for California, and that I had been given a slip by my counselor, and that I had tried to drown someone and was afraid to return to school. Then I remembered what Arthur had said about my being almost grown up and my problems being my own, and I walked around to the back door and went straight up to my room.

I closed the door and sat down on my bed. What I would have to do, I decided, was quit lifesaving and avoid my locker for a while, maybe indefinitely—I could carry all my books with me or leave some of them at home. Beyond that, I would have to take my chances. I understood, but could not put into words, what giving up karate would mean: that my body would never be my own—it could not be my own when it could be taken from me so easily, as it had on that day I'd been attacked. Since that day I'd wanted a power that would extend from the outer layer of my skin down through all my flesh and bones to the very center of myself.

Sitting on my bed, I went over other solutions: getting a dog, or mace, a knife, a gun. But I had already considered these possibilities; I saw again that none of them was good enough. I couldn't bring a dog to school or, later, to a job, and even if I carried a weapon everywhere, it could be taken from me. To be safe every moment, I needed a strength that would remain with me even if I were alone and my hands were empty.

My legs ached and my chest felt hollow. It felt as if something tangible had escaped from me. I had so wanted to be able to defend myself—to defend myself to the last degree. I had wanted to learn to fight so well that I'd achieve what Mr. Park said was possible: the invincible air that would prevent danger from approaching me.

I lay down on my bed and closed my eyes, and in my mind Mr. Park's foot flashed in a sweeping round kick, carving, in the air between us, a circle as large as himself. Then Mr. Park was on both feet again, as still as if he hadn't moved, the circle he had carved enclosing his body, and his mind and his heart.

First Day

You'd think that this was an ordinary day and that we were an ordinary family. The four of us are sitting on dining room chairs. We're sitting down to breakfast. It's Saturday, and after we eat, we're going downtown to the farmer's market.

Looking at Danny now, cutting into a link of sausage, a stranger wouldn't know that his color hasn't fully returned or that he's still much thinner than he was before the accident. Seeing only what's above the table, someone who didn't know Danny wouldn't guess that he'd been in an accident, or be able to tell that, besides wheeling up and down our driveway and occasionally around the block, he hasn't been outside the hospital or this house in three months. But today people at the market, people who don't know Danny, are going to see what's below the table. It was bad enough in the hospital corridors, where patients in wheelchairs are a common sight. Strangers would look at Danny, and then they would look away, and then they would act as if they could not see him.

"As if it matters what you wear to the market!" Zachary, our fifteen year old, says. A few minutes ago, I shouted to Rose from the top of the stairs that the last pair of socks in my drawer was mismatched, and now my two youngest sons are having fun at my expense. What Zachary says is true; half the shoppers at the market dress heedlessly. Many of them are recent immigrants, or poor, or both. I wonder if Rose and I thought of taking Danny down there today, for his first day out in public, because so many of the people there are outside the norm.

"It wouldn't even matter if you wore those socks to work," Zach continues. "Danny, what do you think would be worse: the old man wearing one black and one very dark brown sock to the market, or him wearing those same horribly mismatched socks to work?"

Danny cuts through the yolks of his eggs, and the yellow liquid runs out like blood. "To work," he answers. "At the market, he's anonymous, so it doesn't really matter if he's mistaken for a bag man. But at work, he's known, and his patients would suffer when they realized they'd put their trust in a shrink who can't even dress appropriately."

Zachary laughs, his voice as low as a man's, his control unmistakably a boy's.

Danny stares mock-somberly at his plate. "Either place, he would lose respect, but at work, he could lose maybe even his job." He looks up from his demolished eggs and grins at me. "Right, old man?"

"Right," I say, returning his smile but not his banter because I can't think of anything funny to say. Even these days Danny is rarely at a loss. Sometimes, once his and Zachary's friends are all laughing, Danny will say, "That's a real knee-slapper, hah, hah, hah," rocking back and forth in his chair, and he'll go to slap one of his knees, "hah, hah, hah . . . oh. That's right." And he'll stare down with mock-surprise at the empty space, his hand arrested in midslap. I'll look at his face closely then, thinking, Is his attitude an act? Or is he really so comfortable about it that he can joke like that? He's certainly more comfortable than everyone else. Like in the hospital, when I was trying to tell him about his right leg, that it was too infected. His left leg was already gone. And his right leg was gangrenous, it was dead. And I was struggling for the words to tell him, and he said, so gently, trying to make it easier for me, "Yeah, I know, Dad, it has to come off."

At the time, because he still had the one leg, that one side of him, though it was all shot to hell, still looked pretty much whole, and so he still looked like himself. But afterward, after the second amputation, he came out of recovery, and he was just a torso. I thought, My God, what did they do to my boy? He was smiling groggily. I had to go in the bathroom and stifle my crying. He was so small, he was like a baby.

"Danny!" Zachary says. "Why don't you loan Dad a pair of *your* socks! Why don't you *give* him a pair—or the whole drawerful!"

"I would if I could, but I'm saving those," Danny answers.

"What for?" I ask, caught off guard.

"Sock puppets," Danny says.

I can't help smiling. Rose, also smiling, gets up and starts stacking the plates. Danny swings from the dining room chair onto his wheelchair, rearranges his cut-off pants legs with his hands, and wheels out of the house with Zachary following him. Rose and I carry the breakfast things out to the kitchen.

Near the stove, Rose turns to me with a stricken look. Thinking that all this is finally catching up with her, I set the plates down on the counter and try to take her in my arms. But she pushes me away. "Ralph!" she says. "Do you remember that man we used to see at the market? With the very high amputations?"

I don't know what she's talking about.

"He always wore an army jacket, even in summer," Rose says. "He'd lie on a little table with a cup beside him."

"Oh Christ!" I say. "I totally forgot about him."

"I don't want Danny to see him."

"No," I agree. We both stare at the wooden butcher block, which is hardly smaller than the table at the market on which we've seen the man, lying on his back, shoppers swarming past on either side. Once I put five dollars in the cup, and he lifted his head and called "God bless you" after me. He looked to be about forty years old. Probably was a Vietnam vet. "Wait," I say, remembering. "He hasn't been down there in a couple of years."

"Are you sure?"

"Yes, I'm positive. Not in two years at least."

Rose frowns vaguely, thinking it over. "You're right," she says. She picks up a plate as if it were glass and rinses the bright smear of yolk. I wonder what's happened to the man, if he's someplace better now or worse.

Out in the driveway, Danny transfers from his wheelchair into the back seat, and Zachary folds the chair up, stows it in the trunk, and gets in beside his brother. Rose and I take our seats up front, with me at the wheel, and I reverse down the driveway, turn out of our neighborhood, zoom onto the Jeffries Freeway.

Rose sits beside me so coolly, the shoulder belt dividing her breasts, her shoulders relaxed, her face remarkably calm. That night after the second amputation she cried for hours, like an animal; high, inhuman sounds. And I held her and I talked to her and she wouldn't, she couldn't stop.

Danny's been as calm through the whole thing as his mother is now. I hope he cries when he's alone. He's been unnaturally calm. That one time in the hospital was a relief: after two weeks on his back, one leg already gone, begging us to borrow a wheelchair and give him a ride down the corridors. "I've got to get out of bed. Please. Or just let me sit up." And then, finally starting to cry, "Are they going to fix this goddamn leg or not? Because if they're not, I wish they'd cut the stupid thing off. I don't even care if I keep it anymore, I just want to know what they're going to do." He wept often that day, hugging his best friend and his two older brothers.

And there was one other time, one night last week, when he allowed us on the other side of his calm. Rose and I had just come in from buying milk and steaks for dinner. Danny was sitting in the family room, watching one of those awful sitcoms full of clever yet stupid banter. "How can you watch that garbage?" I asked.

"I'm not," Danny said. "I'm just waiting for the commercials."

I laughed and looked at the set: two teenagers and their father grinning and talking, all glowing with perfect health.

"Dad," Danny said, "want to see what I wrote? Mom, you can look at it, too." And he passed us his dark blue journal, holding it open at its most recent pages. After five two-line entries of who had visited him and what he had eaten for dinner each day he'd written, *It's unfair. This is just so unfair.* I was trying to think of some way to answer him when he said, "I don't want to talk about it, Dad. I just wanted to show it to you." And he wheeled to the stairwell and swung down from his chair and swung up the stairs to his room.

In high school, he used to run up those stairs singing the same line every day: "My momma told me I was great!" He was the captain of the swim team, an honors student, the clown of every class. At U of M, though his grades dipped slightly, he seemed, impossibly, even happier—he loved making new friends, playing intramural basketball, living away from home.

His third year at Michigan is supposed to start in one week. He's set his sights on being back for winter term. Every day he lifts weights and eats red meat and drinks juice laced with wheat germ and brewer's yeast.

The market is crowded, and it takes forever to park. I'm worried that it's so crowded. We came here often with all five kids when they were young, bought them honey-pops and sugarcane to keep them happy while we shopped, but I realize once we're out of the car that none of the kids has come down here in years: the three oldest are on their own, and Danny and Zach have better things to do on summer Saturdays. About once a month, Rose and I come down here by ourselves. We haven't since the day Danny's legs were crushed.

They were crushed in a cardboard carton compactor the first week of his summer job. He was goofing around and fell in. An electronic eye turned the machine on, and the bar started sweeping across. Danny tried to boost himself out, but his feet caught in some boxes, they kept slipping down the walls. The walls of the bin were eight feet high. Danny was six feet tall. He managed to pull himself most of the way out. If he hadn't, he wouldn't be alive.

We're just standing here in the parking lot. I turn to Rose. "So, do we have a lot to buy?"

"Oh," she says. "No, I don't think so." Worry has finally broken out on her face, but it's still distant and detached. Zach's joking smile is gone. He looks ready to defend his big brother at the slightest provocation. Only Danny appears unperturbed. He's as calm as if he hasn't been touched.

"We'll split up," I say. "Zach, you go with your mother and buy vegetables; Danny and I will shop for fruits."

Rose starts to move away from us, calling back automatically, "Don't buy too much."

"Okay," Danny answers. "Don't buy tomatoes."

Rose turns completely around and studies Danny's face as if he has offered her an obscure but important bit of wisdom. She stands motionless until Zachary places his hands on her shoulders and slowly rotates her away from us. "Catch you later," Zach calls, sliding his arm across his mother's back. "Don't buy any . . . any . . . *any corn*," he finishes weakly, unable to think of a vegetable that we might mistake for a fruit.

Danny and I start across the parking lot in the opposite direction Zach and Rose have taken, Danny gracefully reaching back and grabbing his pushrims and thrusting forward. He's ahead of me—already he can move in his chair faster than I can walk. But it's not going to be easy for him to maneuver through the crowds. I stop walking. Danny doesn't see me, and he keeps wheeling toward the huge barnlike building immediately ahead of us until I call him. His wheels glint as he spins around. He returns to me. "We don't have to go in there," I say, gesturing beyond the arched, open doorway to the thronged aisles inside. "It's not going to be any fun for you to maneuver through those crowds."

Danny fingers his pushrims and looks at the people milling along the aisles between the tables of produce. "That's where they sell everything, right?" he says.

I grudgingly say yes.

"Then c'mon. If they don't move fast enough, I'll just mow them down."

I wince at his choice of words, but Danny doesn't see my distorted face; he's already turned around and on his way, reaching, grabbing, and thrusting his pushrims with skill and strength.

Even before we're in the building, people see him. They see what still looks shocking to me at times. Danny's legs end at midthigh. The stumps, pretty much healed now, are wrapped with Ace bandages to help them shrink evenly, and they're also covered by Danny's cut-off pants legs. Neither the bandages nor the flesh shows. But it's what's missing that looks bad, it's looking and seeing nothing where legs are supposed to be that takes your breath away.

I walk beside Danny but a little behind him, aware of the stares and the attempts not to stare, first the shock, the glance down or away, and then the return to face forward, the recovering, the covering up. I'm aware of all this though I'm avoiding looking directly at these people because I don't want to incite them further or get angry in front of Danny. Danny notices the faces, too, but he looks beyond them, at the tables of produce, at the people behind the tables busily hawking. A red-faced man holding up a head of purple cabbage shouts, "C'mon, you people, two for only a dollar!"

"I wonder if all vegetable sellers look like their vegetables," Danny says, his tone a pretty successful attempt at bravado. "No, there's a man selling lettuce, but he looks like a rutabaga. What was that movie? Oh, *Watermelon Man*—hey Dad, let's buy some watermelon."

"Okay. Tell me if you see some."

"I'll keep my eyes peeled," Danny says. "Like grapes. Like oranges. Like potatoes."

Like all these people staring at my boy, I think. I don't mean to notice her, but this young, pretty woman sees Danny and stops walking, she stands still and stares, and I can't help it, I stare back at her so threateningly that she looks even more unsettled before averting her gaze. Seconds later I hear the voice of a boy: "Dad, look! That man doesn't have any— But Dad!" I see the child peripherally, a blond four year old, his father dragging him along so swiftly that he's stumbling and airborne at once.

I don't realize I've stopped walking until Danny looks over his shoulder at me. He's smiling, but his eyes are scared. I step up to him quickly. Before I can speak he says, "Look up there." I follow his finger to the high, beamed ceiling thick with dust and cobwebs and pigeons. I realize that pigeons have been cooing all the while and making that soft, staccato drumming sound as they flutter from beam to beam. Danny and I watch the pigeons' criss-crossing flights and listen to their cooing and the soft beating of their wings. When we start moving again I look at the ground, at the dirty, trash- and produce-littered cement, determined to remain calm.

We reach the end of the building, and I ask the last hawker, a tall man about thirty-five years old, selling mushrooms, if he knows where I can find someone selling watermelons. A moment after I ask the question I realize that the man I've just spoken to is black, though his skin is no darker than mine. Immediately I feel my face growing hot for having asked a black man where to find watermelon. But he seems used to people responding awkwardly to him—he pretends he hasn't noticed the inelegance of my question or my rapid weighing of his coloring and features, and he gives me the directions neither generously nor grudgingly. After he finishes he looks at Danny and asks, "How's it going?" in a tone that's deeper than before and more solicitous. The man is unsmiling but not grave. He looks into Danny's eyes easily, without locking his gaze there.

"Not bad," Danny says. "How about with you?"

"Not bad, either."

I reach into my pocket, pull out my wallet, have it open, the bills halfway out, when I remember that mushrooms are not fruit. Danny sees my hesitation and laughs. "Two pounds," I say. "No, make that three."

"That's a lot of mushrooms," the man says, grabbing up handfuls of them and stuffing them into a big paper bag. "These things are light." He tosses a huge mushroom into the air and catches it.

"We cook a lot of Chinese food," I say.

"We eat them like apples," Danny says. He pats my arm and catches the mushroom seller's eye. "The old man always goes overboard."

The mushroom seller laughs and stuffs the bag full, and I pay him and we move on with him calling "Take it easy" after us in his deep and friendly voice.

The watermelon stall is in the farthest building. On our way to it we pass the place where the man used to lie begging. The man and the table are gone. The space is empty, nothing there but dirty concrete.

The watermelon seller is a white man my age with small, squinty eyes and cuts from shaving on the wrinkled skin of his throat. He looks dismayed when he sees Danny and then terribly upset, as devastated as if Danny were his own son and the accident had just happened today. The watermelon seller lowers his gaze pretty quickly. Danny lowers his, too, dissembling, as he's always done when in trouble since he was a little kid. Suddenly he seems too pale and thin, too obviously and too recently a victim to be out in public. I point peremptorily at the nearest big watermelon.

But the watermelon seller won't let me buy it—he won't take my money. He just shakes his head, pushes my hand away, and places the watermelon in my arms without a word. I feel a surge of emotion—love, joy, grief—and suddenly I'm grateful for everything. I want to tell this man that things aren't as bad as they look, that our lives are becoming livable again. I want him to know how tremendously lucky I feel—just to have Danny, just to *have him*. I try to convey this by thanking the man confidently and looking him in the eyes, but he won't meet my gaze, and if he did I don't think he'd believe me.

We're in the crowds again, heading in the direction we came. I'm carrying the watermelon in my arms. The bag of mushrooms is riding on Danny's lap, though I don't remember him taking it from me.

"We forgot to say when or where we'd meet Mom and Zachary," Danny says.

"Oh Christ!" I say, and I feel helpless all over again.

"I suppose they'll turn up at the car sooner or later," Danny says. He's thrusting his pushrims more slowly now. He's tiring out. As if there were magnets in my hands, I feel the pull of his chair handles. I want to send the watermelon into the legs of the people behind us, then let my hands rise to the back of Danny's chair, grip the handles, lean, and push. I can sense with my whole aching body how good it would feel to propel him along. But even if my hands were free, I couldn't do it. I tried it on the day we left the hospital. Danny's maneuvering was somewhat awkward then, and he was weak, but he possessed enough skill and strength to move in his chair by himself. But I wasn't sure of that, and I wanted to help him, and I thought he could use my help. So I took hold and began pushing him. And Danny frowned, gently, over his shoulder at me and, without saying a word, struck my hands away.

Near tables of broccoli and greens we come upon a dense crowd of people extending the entire width of the aisle. If I were by myself I'd simply thread my way through, but Danny's chair is too wide. I feel like taking Danny in my arms, shouting at these fools to move, and forcing my way into their midst and beyond. But instead we wait, facing the crowd, watching for an opening.

Waiting

I shift my weight on the high hospital bed, take a quick, deep breath, and let it out like steam. Ray looks up. "How are you doing?" he asks. He's sitting across the room on a blue plastic chair, a tan lunch tray abandoned on his knees.

"I'm doing fine," I say, meeting Ray's gaze, trying to gauge how he's feeling. But it's as if he's a lover I haven't yet learned to read. "Come check out your kid," I say. "He's moving just a little—stretching, I think." Ray sets aside the lunch tray and walks over to the bed. During my first pregnancy, Ray would rest his hands on my belly, he would press his cheek close, and also his lips. But now Ray only touches my belly with his fingers, and his touch is light, and his smile is like a ghost's.

Ray returns to his chair, and I look at the VCR screen, at a tape on breastfeeding that a nurse has put in. Filling the screen is a softly smiling mother and her nursing, contented child; the baby is alert, gazing into its mother's eyes.

Dr. Cal reappears in the doorway and says, "Annie? Ray? We can have an operating room at two-thirty. How would you like to meet your baby half an hour from now?" Ray and I nod and smile. All three of us are grinning as if we're about to open some big gift; inside me, where the gift lies, a contraction begins. It feels as if a giant hand is spreading there, thrusting outward through all my flesh, the huge fingers pressing too hard, threatening to hurt me badly, but holding back for now. The threat of worse to come makes me think of the last time I gave birth, and it's as if a shark has risen into sunny water, swimming up from lightless depths. Dr. Cal and Ray don't seem aware of the threat right now. Maybe they're just pretending to be oblivious of it. I keep smiling, pretending to be oblivious, too. But I remind myself not to get too happy, that there's power here far beyond our control.

Dr. Cal leaves the room, taking Ray with him, and two green-clothed women walk in and get to work. They help me into a gown, insert an IV needle into my right hand, tape that hand and arm to an IV board, and strap the board to the bed. "You ladies move fast," I say, trying to get them to look at me. "I feel like I'm at a car wash." The women smile but don't meet my eyes; they're too busy. They shift their hands to the base of my big belly and wash and then shave the top of my pubic hair, where the incision will be made. The scar from last time is still noticeable. The knife will enter at the same place.

But this will not be like the last time, I'm almost sure, although we are at greater risk.

Ray and I haven't talked much about it. It's as if we're on separate boats heading for the same shore. I'm holding my boat steady, Ray's holding his. It's all that we can do for now, almost more than we can do. Later we'll meet up again, when this is all over. Meanwhile our boats surround us like empty shells. Dr. Cal flutters above our bows like a bird and flies ahead toward where the shore will be, if it is there.

———————

The two green-clothed women drape a sheet over my out-stretched legs and big belly and tuck it tightly all around so I can't move. But I tell them to leave my left arm free—I want it to hold the baby—and they do as I say, they leave my arm unrestrained and outside the sheet. Last time both of my arms were tied down, and they took the baby away without letting me see her. This time everything will be different, I tell myself again, and I think of the child I dreamed.

He was sitting on my kitchen counter with red sunlight washing over him. The light rippled like water, its redness turning him pink. He was sitting up by himself. He looked healthy and strong. I woke up feeling someone had made me a promise. My promise dream, I call it in my head, my true dream, even though I don't always believe in it.

When I told the dream to Ray, lying beside him in bed, Ray didn't say anything. I could feel him holding himself somewhere far off. We've lived together for five years, since we were twenty-one and eighteen, but it's felt to me this past year as if we've been living apart.

Last fall, two months after the birth, we took a trip to Isle Royale, a gift from my parents intended to give us solace and time alone together to help us regroup. My parents arranged for lodging and meals for a week, but Ray and I left at the end of the third day. To me, each day on the island felt seamed in by sadness, a pouch of sadness that enclosed all the land, lake, and sky, but I felt better there than I did at home. Still, nothing I said could convince Ray to stay. As soon as we reached the island, my menstrual cycle resumed, and Ray was afraid I might be pregnant again and miscarrying. I tried to assure Ray that I was all right, but Ray didn't trust my judgment or our luck. He felt panicky, he said. Even if I weren't miscarrying, so many other things could go wrong, with me or with him. Anything could happen, and the nearest hospital was half an hour away by plane. I pointed out that we had been far more isolated four years ago while back-packing in British Columbia, but Ray only said, "Yes, I know that. I didn't realize the risk we were taking."

———————

The green-clothed women finish their prep work, and an orderly wheels me to the elevator and takes me down to the basement, leaving me by myself in a windowless hall. All I have to do now is wait. I've already waited nine months, plus the nine months of my other pregnancy, and the three months between; a few more minutes will be easy, I think.

As if to contradict me, a contraction begins, the same huge hand stretching and probing now, pressing too hard. The hand feels vicious, as if it wants to hurt me and also to test me, to see how much stirring up, how much messing with I can take. It makes me think of the hand of a torturer, and I wonder how such a feeling of evil can be part of the beginning of life. I think of the child I dreamed, and now that pink light washing over his skin makes me think of water tinted with blood. I think of that pink, bloody light covering my child and make myself stop. I decided at the beginning of this pregnancy that I wouldn't cry anymore, and for the past nine months I've managed to keep myself steady. Just wait, I remind myself now, looking around at the brown basement walls, the pipes running along them up near the ceiling. It's so quiet down here, buried beneath the earth, as if the surgeons chose this place to help them with cutting downward and inward.

———————

Another pair of green-clothed women appear on either side of my cart. The taller one touches my strapped right hand, checking the IV tube; the other one lifts my free left arm, holding it up for the taller one to see. "Oh, that should have been restrained," the taller woman says.

I want to pull my arm away, but there's nowhere to hide it. The short woman starts to tie a strap around my wrist. "Don't," I say. "My doctor said I could have it free."

"We're tying it loosely, see?" the tall blond woman answers.

"I can't have it tied at all," I say. "I'm going to use it to hold the baby after he's born."

The short woman hesitates; she doesn't knot the cloth.

"You're not going to hold your baby anyway," the tall woman says, not realizing the threat in her words. Again I feel the shark swim up, the water turning nightmare black. "Caesarean babies are taken immediately to the nursery," the tall woman explains. "And if your arm isn't restrained during the operation, you might contaminate the sterile field. You don't want to contaminate the sterile field, do you?"

"I'm not going to," I say. "I'm—"

"Well then it has to be tied."

The tall woman and I continue to argue, in level voices. The woman keeps asking me if I want to contaminate the sterile field; I keep telling her that I'm going to keep my arm out of the way of the operation and that I have my doctor's permission to have my arm free.

We've drawn an audience of green-clothed people: six or seven of them stand in a loose half-circle around my cart. I know that my arm will have to be untied before the operation so the anesthetist can inject the spinal, but I'm afraid that once I'm tied down, though they'll free me for a moment, they'll tie me right up again afterward. With the last birth, that's how it went, in rapid steps—no, in leaps—from a natural birth, to a standard Caesarean, to being knocked out without my permission or even my knowledge, to never seeing my baby at all.

Finally the tall woman says, "Well, you can talk it over with your doctor when you see him. For now that arm is going to have to be tied." The short woman knots the strap, and the green-clothed onlookers look disappointed. Everyone walks away. I lift my arm like a dog testing its leash. There are three inches of strap between my wrist and the bed rail. My other arm, taped to the IV board and strapped to the other rail, is completely immobile, as are my legs, belly, and feet, bound by the deeply tucked sheets. The hand inside me tightens into a fist, then spreads its fingers and digs, and digs deeper. Again I feel the shark. He's so close I can't tell where he is.

I'm wheeled to the operating room, where a fat, fair-skinned nurse and a dark, wiry anesthetist are waiting for me. The nurse untucks the sheets and methodically unties the arm that the other women and I just made such a fuss over. Then the nurse and the anesthetist help me onto my side. "Do your best to get into a fetal position," the nurse says.

I curl around my big belly and close my eyes tight, and the anesthetist walks his fingers down my spine, feeling for a good place to insert the needle. A cold wet spot appears on my back, and I smell alcohol. "So," the anesthetist says in a chatty voice, "how many children do you have at home?"

I feel as if I've been struck. I lose my breath. Then my body convulses, and I can't hold back my sobs.

I can sense the nurse and the anesthetist beyond the wall of my crying, beyond my heaving body; they're waiting for me to stop, or to explain myself, or for a clue about what they can do. I know that they must have a good idea of why I'm crying, but suddenly I need to tell them; I can hardly speak, but I want to pull the truth out of the dark. The words come out of me in pieces: "My—one—baby—died."

I don't realize that I've been gone until I come back, to the sound of my crying, and the weight of two soft hands pressing my shoulder and my hip, and two leaner, harder hands resting against my back and the back of my neck. It feels as if they're holding me together.

The nurse suggests I try breathing deeply and slowly, and I try it and it works. It's as if I'm learning to breathe for the first time; all I hear and feel is my own breath as it leaves and enters my body. "Okay," I say. "I'm ready now."

Again I curl in on myself as far as I'm able. The anesthetist fingers my spine, and the cool wet spot reappears. "Hold perfectly still now," he says. There's a pause, an absolute stillness.

I don't feel the needle going in, but the anesthetist says "Finished," and he and the nurse help me onto my back. The nurse reties the arm strap quickly, unthinkingly, as if she were retying a shoe. Then she goes to the door and lets in a group of green-clothed people, among them Ray and Dr. Cal.

As soon as all of them have taken their places, I raise my left arm the few inches that the strap allows. "Can I have this arm free?" I ask, looking into Dr. Cal's eyes, the only part of him not hidden by cloth.

Dr. Cal looks over my head, and I can tell that his friendly, piercing gaze is looking right into the anesthetist. "What do you say, Doctor?" Dr. Cal says. "You're never going to get a better patient."

This might be a lie. I don't know how I'll react. Dr. Cal wasn't at the last birth. The doctor who was knocked me out seconds afterward, before I could suspect that something was wrong.

The anesthetist must nod or shrug his agreement. Dr. Cal picks up my wrist, and, with a scalpel that has appeared in his hand like magic, he slices the strap in two with one stroke. I take Ray's hand in mine and face the cloth screen rising above me and the table. Now things will move fast. Now the waiting is as close as it can be to being over.

A scalpel stings across me like a fingernail tracing a line; then the whole inside of my belly is moving as if the baby is wrestling with the doctor's hands. It doesn't hurt, but it's frightening; it feels too powerful, more than my body can bear. Then a sudden, tremendous absence exists, as if someone has knocked me hollow.

"It's a girl," someone says; *a girl*, I think, and before I can ask to see her, she is being held above me. Her skin is a bright, deep blue, the way the sky gets sometimes in fall, on the clearest, most brilliant of days. I can see right away that she's healthy and strong. Ray sees it, too; he says into my ear, "She looks good, Annie, she looks really good."

The baby is twisting and struggling in the doctor's hands, crying and fighting the bulb syringe suctioning liquid from her mouth. The bulb syringe follows her struggling head, and she twists the other way, breaking free.

Beneath the baby's crying, I notice a strange sound, coming

from somewhere close. It's a sound like I've never heard, human and inhuman, stranger than the blueness of my daughter's skin. I listen to it with no idea of what it is until I realize that it's coming from me: a low, keening moan; sad, hopeless, inconsolable; but what makes it so strange is that it isn't sustained—it starts and it stops, broken by my laughter.

My baby stops crying and is placed in my arm. She's breathing deeply and beginning to turn pink; pink is overtaking the blue, starting from the center of her chest and spreading outward, washing over her like water, like light.

Sophie's Shirt

The patchwork shirt I pieced while pregnant with Sophie was too large for her to be buried in, so I put the shirt away in a drawer I rarely opened. Sometimes looking for something else I happened upon it and glanced at it without emotion: it was just a piece of clothing. Other times seeing it I startled as if I'd come across a body, or my eyes suddenly stung and I began crying. More than once I found myself marveling at all of the work that had gone into it—the shirt is made of tiny gold, blue, red, and off-white squares, all stitched by my own hands.

At times I have thought of loaning the shirt: to my first niece, to my second niece, to the babies of friends. Four years after Sophie's death, my second daughter found the shirt and pulled it onto one of her dolls. *Maybe that's the best use for it,* I thought. But coming across it on the floor one day, I picked it up, smoothed and folded it, and placed it out of sight on the high shelf where it lies now.

In bed one night I think of the shirt. *What am I going to do with it?* I think. *It's been five years.* And I drift toward sleep. Suddenly I am wide awake and racing with energy, flooded with longing and joy mixed with pain. An image has jolted me from half-sleep, an image sharper than the clearest of dreams: it's a coffin with me inside it, white-haired and shriveled, unrecognizably aged. I know it's me only because Sophie's shirt is lying with me, in the hollow between my body and my arm.

The End
of the
Crackhead

My brother Arthur is standing in the doorway of my ex-husband's house, where he is staying, instead of with me, because I have moved to a tiny apartment. Arthur's dark blond hair is pulled back from his face, and he is wearing a sweat-shirt and jeans and black All Stars, the only kind of shoes he's worn since I was eleven and he was twelve. "Want to watch me burn this?" he calls as I step out of my car; he is holding up, with both hands, a long box made of yellowish wood. "The fire's ready," he says. "We waited for you in case you wanted to watch."

"Yeah, Mom, what *took you so long*?" my daughter asks, appearing behind Arthur at the top of the steps.

"I'm not late," I say. "I'm supposed to pick you up at five o'clock, and it's a few minutes to five right now."

"Oh, don't listen to *Marly*," Arthur says, poking at her head with an elbow, since his hands are taken up by the box. "She's been bugging me to burn this since daybreak."

"What is it?" I ask. Arthur has told me that he's been working on a project, but he hasn't said what it is; "I'll show it to you when I finish it," he's said.

I walk toward them up the sandy path, and as I reach the front stoop Arthur tilts the box toward me, and I see that what he's holding is a coffin—a child-size coffin with a clear glass lid. In a flash I think of my first child, who died the same day she was born—she was placed in a coffin about this same size—but I put her out of my mind when I see what's inside the coffin that Arthur has made. Behind the glass lies a figure of reddish clay that looks like a cross between a gargoyle and a person. Its scrawny body rests with its hands at its sides as if laid out by a mortician, but its mouth is wide open, in a scream of terror or pain. I stare through the glass lid, drawn to and repelled by the figure's agonized expression.

"It's a crackhead," Arthur says.

"It's what Uncle Arthur looked like when he was on drugs," Marly explains.

I stare at the crackhead's rough, orange-red skin, at its stunted forehead, and at its empty, eyeless sockets; then I return to its open mouth, its lips peeled back from its teeth in a frozen scream. The figure—the creature—looks nothing like Arthur, but its desperate mouth makes me think of a phone call Arthur made to me just before the first time he tried to quit drugs. *Please help me, you've got to help me, please help me,* he cried, sounding more terrified than I've ever heard anyone sound.

Shortly after that phone call, Arthur came to live with me and my husband in the house on whose steps we now stand. In the evenings, Arthur sat on these steps with Marly, watching the birds that flew down to our feeder. Marly was three then. She taught Arthur the birds' names. Arthur stayed with us then for a little more than a month; he stayed off drugs for a little more than a year.

I look away from the crackhead to its surrounding frame of

woods: white oak oiled yellow and inlaid with black walnut. Arthur keeps the coffin still, letting me look for as long as I like. "I *want* to say it's beautiful," I finally say. Arthur laughs. "The *coffin* is beautiful. The crackhead is . . . it's gruesome, but it's really good, Arthur. It's one of the best things you've ever made."

Arthur's mouth turns up slightly with a satisfied smile. He is thirty years old and has been making things from clay ever since his ninth-grade ceramics class.

"Are you sure you want to burn it?" I ask.

"Yup," Arthur says. "Marly, go get your dad and tell him we're ready to start." Marly runs down the steps and across the yard toward the shop.

"Are you going to take it out of the coffin first?" I ask, touching a triangle of black walnut set into the yellowish oak.

"No," Arthur says, his huge eyes mostly hidden by his eyelids, "I'm going to burn the whole thing." He keeps his gaze lowered to the coffin as if embarrassed. "This ritual is very important to me. I hope you don't mind that Marly's here for it."

"I'm not sure if I do," I say, "but I think it's too late now to make her stay in the house."

"I thought of keeping it from her," Arthur says, "but you know how she follows me around—every day that she's over here, from the minute she gets off the bus."

"Don't worry about it," I say.

"She's the only person who loves me that I haven't lied to," Arthur says. He smiles ruefully. "Maybe because she's only six, and I usually only see her once a year, but still, I wanted her to be here."

"That's fine," I say. "She seems fine with it."

As Arthur continues to gaze down at the coffin, I think vaguely, in a quick, dark flash, of the things he's told me in the last few weeks: that he started drinking at twelve and shooting heroin at sixteen, and that he spent his whole adolescence and nearly all his adult life telling lies to conceal his abuse. During this current visit, he's been using words like "evil" and "disgusting" in talking about his past and speaking as if his past self is someone completely different from the person he's so recently become.

"But you weren't *just* an addict," I finally protested one evening as we walked on the beach. I was thinking of how he flew in and took care of me after my first baby's birth and death. Arthur cooked dinner for Ray and me all week and sat by my bed during the day, and on the night before he left he talked me into venturing out of the house again. And I was thinking also, more vaguely, of how, all his life, people have been drawn to Arthur's kind nature and to his charm. "You were more than just an addict," I said. "You were a good person, too, all those years. Everyone liked you. People's faces lit up when you came in the room."

"Yeah, the life of the party," Arthur said, his face tightened into a frown.

"You had a terrific sense of humor," I insisted. "And empathy. You always said the right things."

"That was the drugs talking," Arthur said in a tone that finished the subject.

Now his face is smooth and calm, and he stands without speaking, gazing down at the crackhead as if it's a gift of which he is ashamed, while I stand across from him, not knowing what to say. Finally I ask, "Did you get ahold of Brenda? Is she going to send you some of your clothes?"

"I don't know," Arthur says. "I did call her again last night and ask her to send at least my jacket and a couple pairs of my jeans, but I think probably, eventually, she'll just throw everything out." He sighs, sadly and a little fiercely, and lifts his knee to the bottom of the coffin so he can shift his hands and change his grip. "I don't blame her for not trusting me," he says, "but I *wish* she would give me another chance. Hell, I don't trust myself, either, but I haven't given up on myself."

"You can't afford to," I point out.

"*You* haven't given up on me," he says.

"That's because I'm your sister. I'm not going to give up on you, but I don't trust you, either."

Arthur laughs, angling his head back, bumping the coffin against his thigh; he looks surprised and a little sad, but he also seems somewhat pleased. I think talking about the gravity of his situation lightens some of its weight. And I'm sure it's comforting to him that I haven't abandoned him, and that I probably never will.

Marly returns from the shop with her dad, tugging him along

by his hand. A fine layer of sawdust powders the sleeves of Ray's shirt, and a small wood shaving clings to his beard. We say hi, with a friendly distance I haven't grown used to—we've lived apart for less than a year—and then the four of us walk across the cold grass to a fire blazing at the edge of the yard.

The fire has been built like a funeral pyre, with squared-off layers of crisscrossed logs. Beyond the fire lies the woods in which I used to walk, at first with Ray, and later with Marly or by myself. I look at the oaks and maples and beeches, lit by evening light slanting in from Lake Michigan, and imagine myself standing among those trees again. Pale patches of snow gleam from the wet ground, and I smell the earth and the scent of rotting leaves and the woodsmoke curling away from us.

"Uncle Arthur, can I throw some more boards on?" Marly asks.

"Sure," Arthur says.

Marly begins picking up rectangles and triangles from a pile of scrap lumber and tossing them one by one onto the fire; Ray stands beside her, pointing out pieces she can easily reach. I watch flames engulf a triangular scrap, then turn to look at the crackhead again. As I stare down into the shallow, sealed vault, I feel a hush like the hush inside a church.

The crackhead rests on satiny white cloth littered with curved pieces of broken glass. "What's the glass from?" I ask, almost in a whisper.

"Empty crack vials," Arthur says, also softly. "I had a couple in my pocket when I got to the hospital." Arthur shifts the coffin onto his left hip to free his right hand and points down through the lid. "That piece of blue-and-white-striped cloth near his feet is from my hospital gown, and the scrap of white cloth under his head is from my pillowcase. He's lying on top of my fingernail clippings, a miniature gin bottle, and a swatch of my hair."

I glance at Arthur's pulled-back hair, wondering where he's made the cut, and then I look at his face. He looks better than he did the first time he tried to quit; when he came to stay with Ray and Marly and me then, his eyes made me think of someone who had been tortured and who expected to be tortured again. During this current visit, from the evening three weeks ago when

I picked him up at the airport, Arthur has seemed much less frightened and more sure of himself. But he still seems unhappy and brittle. Besides his girlfriend and nearly all his belongings, he has left behind his chef's job at the Manhattan Sheraton and his classes and sculpture studio at City College of New York, and just last night as we sat on my porch he said that he didn't know if he could return to a place where men drank on the street and he could find crack and heroin for sale as readily as bread and milk.

"What will you do if you don't go back?" I asked.

"I don't know," Arthur said. He was sitting on a chair near the porch light, working on a spoon of lilac wood. "I don't know. I've been saying that a lot lately—'I don't know.' It's a novelty, not always having an answer for everything, not to mention trying to always tell the truth."

"Okay, Marly, that's good," Arthur says now, glancing at her upraised arm. Marly throws on one last piece of wood. The fire snaps, burning fiercely. Arthur sets the coffin on the ground, levels the top of the fire with a long, heavy stick, then picks up the coffin and sets it on the flames. For the first time, I notice that the coffin's lid is secured by a padlocked hasp.

The oiled wood catches quickly, flames licking up all four sides of the box and shooting straight up into the air; then some of the flames begin to bend, to curl inward over the lid, throwing shadows and shifting light on the crackhead's body and face. The crackhead's orange flesh glows beneath the glass, and in the wavering light its strained-wide lips appear to strain a little wider, and then its body seems to move, almost imperceptibly. I'm not sure what it is that I think I might have seen—it feels more as if I've just missed seeing something, missed the shifting of an arm, a shoulder, or a leg. I continue to watch carefully, and again the crackhead seems, maybe, to move just slightly, indeterminately. I know that this is a trick of the firelight and its shadows and of my own mind, that the crackhead cannot shift or stir; still, it looks as if it's about to. And as I continue to stare at its glowing flesh and its eyeless, screaming face, trying to detect either movement or the lack of it, suddenly, as quickly as if a switch has been flipped, my perception is changed—all at once, it looks to me as if the crackhead is actually screaming, and not because of some unnamed agony, but with a greater and more immediate terror: because it can feel and hear the surrounding fire and knows it will be burned alive.

I keep these thoughts to myself so as not to frighten Marly, but her perception is at least similar to mine. "He looks like he's screaming to get out," she says. I put my arm around her shoulders and draw her head in to my waist, but she struggles upright, saying, "No, I want to see." Even as she speaks, flames are streaking across the lid, blackening the glass. Soon the crackhead disappears from our sight.

The four of us stand watching the coffin blaze. "How long will it take?" I ask.

"I don't know," Arthur says. He pokes the coffin with the stick, trying to settle it deeper into the fire, and the end of the stick strikes the padlock, flipping it up and then back down with two sharp taps.

"What if he gets out?" Marly asks.

"He can't," Arthur says. "The coffin's nailed and locked shut. And anyway, Marly, he can't move by himself."

There's a loud pop, like a gun shot, and then the tinkling of breaking glass. "He's getting out!" Marly cries.

All four of us have jumped back from the fire and are staring at the blazing coffin; flames rise from its rim, and from this distance and angle we can't see inside it.

Arthur bends down so that his face is next to Marly's; he encloses her shoulders from behind with his hands and leans his jaw close to her cheek. "No he's not," he says. "He's not going to get out. This is the end of him. I promise."

Within
the
Lighted
City

My parents' apartment door, hung with a wreath of copper bells, stands open to the outer hallway. We walk in, and Marly drops her boots on the tiled floor of the inner hall and runs down the corridor to the computer room. As I set down the rest of our stuff (our ancient suitcase, my running shoes, my books, and a bag of presents), I hear my brothers talking from the other direction, and I'm so eager to see them that I straighten up and walk toward them without stopping to take off my coat. They look up at me, the four of them sprawled on the white leather couches and chair. "Nice coat, Annie," Dan says with surprise.

Arthur stirs in his chair and mumbles something, and my other three brothers laugh.

"What?" I ask the group of them. "What did you say?" I ask Arthur, walking over to the chair across which his lanky body is draped.

"Never mind," Arthur says, his face slightly peeved, a look designed, I'm sure, to milk more humor from his remark.

"C'mon, *tell* me," I say, pushing Arthur's knee with my hand. "What did you say about my coat? What's wrong with it?" I really want to know what Arthur thinks; he's a year older than me, and, even though I'm thirty-one, I still tend to look up to him. Maybe the coat is too old-fashioned, too long, or maybe the flared cut is a little extreme. Or maybe it's too gaudy. It's fake cherry red, the color of a maraschino.

"Nothing's wrong with it," Arthur says.

"Then what did you say about it?"

Dan, who is twenty-nine, leans toward me from the couch. "He said, 'Yeah, well, I still want to see the receipt.'" Mike and Zachary laugh again, it seems in homage to the original delivery.

I turn back to Arthur. "What do you mean—are you saying that I stole it?"

"No, no," Dan says. "He meant that you got it at the Salvation Army or somewhere."

I go over the exchange in my head: *Nice coat, Annie; Yeah, well, I still want to see the receipt.* "They give receipts at the Salvation Army," I say.

This brings a loud laugh from Zachary, my youngest brother. At six feet three inches and two hundred pounds, Zach is also the largest of my brothers, but I used to take care of him when I could lift him up by his armpits, and when he sees me looking at him sternly he explains, "You're completely familiar with how the Salvation Army operates."

Finally it's becoming clear to me what this whole thing is about: my brothers are teasing me for being so cheap. I don't think they've stopped to consider that, while I've been cheap all my life, since my divorce and return to school my habitual scrimping has become a necessity.

"Tell the truth, Ann," Dan says. "Did you buy it new?"

"No, but I didn't buy it at the Salvation Army. I bought it at this second-hand store that has a lot nicer stuff."

"What did I tell you?" Arthur says, and he sets his lips in a stiff line and folds his arms across his chest.

"Well, what's wrong with that?" I ask. "Like you're Mr. GQ." I push Arthur's foot this time, and he resettles it to the floor. He is wearing his usual art student clothes: paint- and glaze-spattered gym shoes and T-shirt and jeans.

"We were just having fun with you, Nini," Mike, my oldest brother, says. "It's a pretty coat, and it looks really nice on you."

"Well, thanks," I say. I throw a glare sidelong at Arthur.

"I never said it wasn't nice," Arthur says.

"Maybe I'll go hang it up now, unless someone has something to add."

"Nope," Dan says, "I think that was it. But wait a minute, let me check—"

I walk back to the hallway and unbutton my coat. I bought it a week ago, to wear for Toby. He hasn't seen me in it yet. We live on opposite sides of the state, and though we've been corresponding for two and a half years, I've only seen him once in that time: we met for lunch north of Detroit near the high school where Toby teaches, ten weeks after the summer conference at which Toby and I first met. At that second meeting, after we ate lunch, Toby and I walked through a chilly park and talked of becoming lovers. He said he couldn't imagine abandoning his wife and his daughter, and though I left my husband partly as a result of meeting Toby, I only wanted to have an affair, I told Toby, if it could lead to marriage. We didn't kiss during that walk, and we kept our hands at our sides. Mine were cold, and I wanted to shove them into the pockets of my down coat, but I kept them out, hoping that Toby would take one in his.

I drove home to my new apartment feeling angry and determined: angry at Toby for inviting me all the way across the state just to reject me, and determined to find love elsewhere. And I did find it, or at least something close to it for a while, first, for a few months, with a fellow student at Western Michigan, and then, for a year and a half, with a married man from Grand Haven who replaced Toby, the man I loved and hoped to marry, until the affair ended. Still, Toby and I continued to write each other, every couple of months during my affair with Lowell, and more frequently after it ended. Our letters were full of warmth and solicitude and occasional flares of anger, our sexual feelings cloaked in friendship or pushed down under the surface.

I thought I had given up on ever becoming Toby's lover. Then, just before I came home for Christmas, Toby wrote me a letter that was different from all the others; he wrote inviting me to lunch while I was in Detroit, and, though he is still married, from the tone of this letter and other things written in it, it seemed that he was inviting me to more than just lunch. I wrote him back that I felt funny about leaving Marly with my family, since they would want to know where I was going and with whom. I could lie to them, of course, but my family is nosy, and I'm not good at hiding the truth, and while I don't care if my brothers know that I'm thinking about starting an affair, I am worried about making my mom feel bad. My dad had an affair years ago through which I watched my mom suffer. It took her years to completely recover. That didn't stop me from having an affair with Lowell, and it might not stop me this time, either, but I don't want to use my parents' apartment as the launching pad for my transgression.

As I hang up my coat in the hall closet, my mom appears at my side. "There you are," she says, giving me a hug and a kiss. "I knew you were here, because Marly came running back." She smiles. "At least I figured Marly didn't get here by herself."

"Good figuring, Mom," I say. Marly is eight, and we've just driven in from Saugatuck, three and a half hours away. "Where's Dad?" I ask.

"At the airport, picking up Grandma."

"He went all by himself?"

"Yeah—Grandma's getting kind of old for a lot of excitement. Ralphy thought it would be more restful if he got her alone." My grandma is eighty-seven. My dad is fifty-eight, a little old to be called Ralphy, but my mom changes everyone's name so that it ends in a long *e* sound. Her children, from the top down, are Mikey, Artie, Annie, Danny, and Zachary. Mike's fiancée, Sarah, is Sary, and Zachary's wife, Sasha, is Sashy. Dan's daughters, Ruth and Greta, are Ruthie and Grettie, and Nicole, my dad's daughter from his affair, is Nicki. Nicole lives with her mother, but she visits "Dad and Rosie," as she calls them, two evenings a week and for parts of the holidays.

"Where's everybody else?" I ask.

"Oh, let me see," my mom says. "I was just showing Sary a computer program for calculus, Sashy's in the bathroom, I think, Marly and Nicki are playing with the dress-up clothes, and I'm not sure where all of your brothers are."

"I know where *they* are. What about Greta and Ruth? Are they going to come after all, or not?"

"No, I guess they're going to stay with their mom, and we'll see them at New Year's."

"She had them last Christmas," I say. "It's Dan's turn."

"I know," my mom says. "But, well, it's up to Danny to stand up for himself."

I rub my mom's back with my palm, simply glad to see her. She's so noninterfering. And she has a genius IQ, yet she says things like "Danny stand up for himself," when Dan hasn't stood in ten years. He's used a wheelchair to get around since he was nineteen, when his legs were severed at a summer factory job.

"Are you hungry?" my mom asks. "We're going to eat as soon as Ralphy and Grandma get here, but do you want a little something to snack on for now?"

"No," I say, "I'll wait."

"Well, I'm going to go see how Sary's doing with that program. I was just getting her started."

My mom returns to the rear of the apartment, and I step from the small, bright square of hallway back into the living room, which is suddenly dark. Someone has turned off the overhead lights as well as the lights of the tree, and one of the white leather couches has been pushed aside to reveal the view out the two walls of windows. My brothers are sitting on the remaining couch and the chair, both of which have been shifted to the center of the room, and the shapes of their bodies are outlined by the white leather glowing around their still forms.

Outside, the night is brightened by the lights of downtown Detroit. We are six stories up, and, looking straight out, all I can see is blackness lit by lights shining from every direction, lower than my parents' windows, and higher, and at the same level. Seeing the darkness lit up without any apparent relation to gravity makes it seem as if the apartment is floating; it feels as if we are hanging suspended in the darkness, above and below and within the lighted city. The soft grayness inside the apartment makes it feel as if I am floating, too, as if I'm not attached to anything.

My spell flits off like a dream when I squeeze between Zachary and Dan. Zachary pats my left thigh, and Dan takes my right hand. We are all lined up facing the river: Zachary, then me, then Dan, then Mike, then Arthur on the chair to our right. Arthur is talking about the Canadian Club sign on Canada's shore, a mile away, which blinks on and off at the far left edge of the windows. It is made of orange neon and blinks with a pulsing rhythm.

"I wonder how many alcoholics have apartments facing that sign," Arthur says. "I wonder how many of them were alcoholics *before* they began reading that sign a thousand times a night. I wonder if I start drinking again, if I can sue Canadian Club."

"Are you worried about starting to drink again?" Dan asks.

"Hell no," Arthur says. "I wouldn't anyway, but what with this other drug I have to take, there's no way."

Arthur is taking fourteen hundred milligrams of Tegretol a day in an attempt to control his epilepsy, which began to surface as faint leg spasms ten years ago and has grown in the two years since he's quit using alcohol and other drugs into seizures that grip and shake his whole body. After a seizure strikes, it takes Arthur a week or longer to recover his energy, and sometimes he stutters for months, and while he hasn't suffered any permanent brain damage, his neurologist says that he likely will if the seizures continue to occur. They keep switching Arthur's medications and upping the dosages. He hasn't had a seizure now for almost three months, but over the summer he lasted three months and one week, and then two seizures struck ten days apart.

"Look at how black the river is," I say. It's a thick, black line dividing Windsor from Detroit.

"There's a boat," Mike says. "All the way to the right."

"Oh, cool," Arthur says. "A barge." The barge has been outlined in lights, as if for Christmas.

"Mmmm, this looks cozy," Sasha says, appearing from around the side of the couch and settling onto Zachary's lap. "Oh, hi, Annie!" She leans down and gives me a kiss. "When did you get in?"

"Just a little while ago."

Zach pats Sasha's butt, then points his huge index finger at the barge. "How often do those pass by?" he asks Arthur. Arthur lives with our parents. Zach and Sasha live in San Diego and only fly back to Detroit once or twice a year.

"Not too often, I don't think," Arthur says. "But then, how often do I sit here looking out? I'm at school or my studio most of the day, and when I'm home I'm usually doing something. Probably all kinds of things happen out there when I'm not looking."

"I know what you mean," Dan says. "Six or seven spaceships were out there when *I* got here today. They were circling the RenCen. One landed on top. Then the other six started shooting it out. Three of them went up in flames and fell into the river. Then the rest of them zoomed off." He looks around at the rest of us. "You didn't see it? Nobody else saw it?" Arthur reaches over from his chair and noogies Dan's part-bald, part-bristly head.

"What are you guys talking about, anyway?" Marly asks. She has slipped around the edge of the couch and is standing in front of Sasha and Zach.

"Hi, Marly!" Sasha says. "Hi, sweetie!" She leans forward and gives Marly a kiss. Marly is wearing a round straw hat tied on with a scarf, with three or four more silky scarves draped around her neck. The rest of her, except for her thin arms and her face, is lost in yards of dark cloth.

"We're talking about flying saucers," Mike says. "Have you ever seen one?"

"*I* haven't," Marly says, "but some people in Saugatuck have. They fly over Lake Michigan at night and blink their lights."

"C'mere, my little-favorite-anorexic *niece*," Dan says, grabbing Marly's wrist.

Marly screeches with delight, and Dan draws her onto his lap.

"Did I ever tell you about this anorexic I met while I was at Cornell?" Arthur asks.

"You make it sound like you went to the university," Dan says. "Why don't you just say, 'When I was locked up for doing drugs'?"

"Actually, I was a walk-in," Arthur says. "The anorexics weren't walk-ins, though. They were all young girls, and their parents had signed them in, at $300 a day."

"You're joking," Mike says.

"It was so expensive because they had to be watched round the clock to make sure they didn't make themselves vomit."

"Oh, gross," Marly says.

"I'm with you," Sasha says. "Marly, come sit on our laps."

Dan tightens his arms around Marly. "No, she's mine, I had her first. Well, all right—go on." He passes Marly, smiling, her legs dragging and the blue cloth trailing, over me to Sasha.

"Speaking of anorexics," Sasha says, "look who could absolutely *not* be mistaken for an anorexic anymore. Darlin', you look gorgeous," she says to Nicole, who is standing in front of us now.

"Thank you," Nicole says. My little sister is thirteen and just beginning to put on a little weight all over, including on her breasts and her hips. She is draped sari-style in shimmering, light cloth, and her head is wrapped in a white turban-style twist.

"Hey, baby, you can come sit on my lap," Arthur says.

"No thanks," Nicole says, patting a yawn. "I think I'll sit on the couch."

"Ha! She knows better already," Zach says.

"Arthur the *lady's* man," Dan says, holding out his hand for Arthur to slap.

"Look who's talking," Arthur says, ignoring Dan's hand. "Or, as Mom would say, 'Look at the pot calling the kettle black.'"

"Hey, don't be putting me in your league, buddy," Dan says. "You're way up there with Wilt the Stilt and Magic Johnson."

"Not anymore," Arthur says. "I've cut way back. And the way you've been adding on, pretty soon you're going to pass me."

"What are you talking about?" Dan says. "I've never even had a one-night stand. I might not be perfect, but I'm not like you— at least I always start out with good intentions."

"Yeah, and I'm sure all the three-month stands you've had since your divorce were thrilled about your good intentions when you blew them off."

"Can you guys change the subject?" I ask, worried about the questions that Marly will ask me later.

"I don't think Arthur's epilepsy is from too much drugs," Dan says. "I think it's from too much sex."

"Thanks for the insight," Arthur says. "I'll pass it on to my neurologist."

"Maybe he can do a study," Dan says. "You can be the sex maniac, and I can be the control."

"C'mon, Dan," I say. "If Greta and Ruth were here, would you be talking like this?"

"Probably," Dan says. Then he looks at me and says, "Okay, sorry."

"*Any*how," Arthur says, "as I was starting to say, I got to know a couple of anorexics at Cornell because when they reach a certain weight they're allowed to play volleyball with the addicts. And this one anorexic told me that she used to come home from school every day, take one Cheerio out of the box, and cut it into eight pieces with an Exacto knife. Then she'd eat each tiny little piece, one at a time, by placing it on the center of her tongue and closing her mouth. She wouldn't chew or swallow. It took fifteen minutes for each eighth of a Cheerio to dissolve, so it took her two hours to eat one Cheerio."

"You're making this up," Zach says.

"This is what she told me," Arthur says. "And she said that when her mom came home, her mom would beg her to eat, and she'd say, 'Mom, I've been eating ever since I got home from school.'"

We all laugh; then Sasha says, "That's sad."

"It's crazy," Marly says. "I eat a whole bowlful of Cheerios at one time."

"Then how come you're so scrawny?" Dan asks.

"Don't call her scrawny," I say. "She's naturally thin. She's perfect."

"Yeah, be quiet, Dan," Arthur says, "or we'll get out those old family slides where you've got those little toothpick arms and legs."

"Well, at least my legs were fatter then than they are now," Dan says, looking down at the space where his lower legs used to be, his hugely muscled upper body angled over what he calls his "nubs": ten inches of thigh whose rounded, healed ends poke out of his cut-off sweats. "Yeah, Marly, don't go on any diets," Dan says. "That's the mistake I made. I was trying to lose just a little off my belly, but, well, I guess my aim was off, plus I got slightly carried away." He looks into Marly's face and attempts a guileless smile.

"What do you think I am, three years old?" Marly says. Over our laughter she asks, "Uncle Dan, can I play in your chair?"

"Don't you think you're a little old for *playing*?" Dan says. "Yeah, you can. But be careful—it's not mine. I'm just test-driving it before I deliver it to a customer."

"Can I use it, too?" Nicole asks.

"Yeah, sure. No popping wheelies, though. You want to goof around, wait till tomorrow, and I'll get you a chair out of my van."

But before the girls get up from our laps, the front door opens loudly. Our dad has always opened doors more loudly than any-one else. "Grandma's here," Mike says.

We listen to the harmonious voices of our grandma and our mom greeting each other. Then our dad's voice booms out: "How come all the lights are off in here?"

Our dad appears before us, a silhouette against our view, the lights from the city outlining the wisps of hair that spring up from his mostly bald head. Though the whole front of him is in darkness, you can still vaguely see his large nose and his chin and the overall intensity of his face. "What did you do with the other couch?" he demands.

"We sold it," Dan says.

"Jesus Christ, how many of you are sitting on one damn couch?"

"Just about the whole damn family," Arthur says.

Dan pats his lap. "There's room for you, Old Man."

Our dad sighs, his body loosening just slightly. Then his nor-mal intensity returns. "*Annie*," he says, with happy surprise. "And *Marly*. It's so dark in here, I didn't see you." He leans down and kisses us. "Well, good, everybody's here then." He turns to-ward the hall. "Rosie! When are we going to eat?"

"*I'm* cooking dinner, Old Man," Arthur says.

"Then what are you doing just sitting around?"

"Enjoying the view, not to mention waiting for you. It's all done, I just need to take it out of the oven."

"Well, take it out of the goddamned oven, I'm starving."

"*Relax*, Old Guy," Arthur says. "You just got here."

"Do they make Ritalin for adults?" Dan asks.

"Quaaludes," Arthur says. "Reds. Alcohol. Heroin."

"I'm going to go say hi to Grandma," Mike says. He stands.

Marly puts her lips to my ear and whispers, "Do I have to kiss her?"

"You don't have to, but it would be nice. Why don't you want to?"

Marly whispers again. "She's so *old*."

"Hey, no secrets around here," Dan says.

"Well then we'll take our secrets elsewhere."

"Before everybody takes off," our dad says, "a couple of you move the couches back where they belong." He flicks on the lights, and everyone stands except for Dan, who hops onto the floor and lifts an arm of the couch.

―――――

All twelve of us are sitting around the rosewood table, which has been extended to its full length so that it fills up the alcove off the living room. We're pretty much wedged into our seats, eating lasagna and passing bread, everyone talking at once. My grandma is sitting across from me and a couple of settings down, and my attention wanders from the table chatter as I watch her. I can see why Marly is afraid to kiss her—as Marly pointed out to me when we retreated to the computer room, my grandma does resemble a dead person. The wrinkled flesh of her face has shrunk close to the bone, as if the skeleton she will become is already emerging, and her normally tan complexion has a faded, yellowish cast, except for her cheekbones, which are colored the same brilliant red as her lips. If she held still and closed her eyes, you could mistake her for a corpse made up by an overzealous mortician.

But my grandma doesn't close her eyes, which are large and one hundred percent lucid, and she doesn't hold still as she eats, and though she moves slowly, her movements are fluid. She is a tiny woman, at four feet eleven inches, four inches shorter than me. We're the two shortest adults in the family, except for Dan, of course, though he was six feet before his accident, and now the immense breadth of his muscled shoulders and chest makes him seem anything but small. Besides being short, I am like my grandma in other ways: thin, dark, and, as Toby has called me, Italianate, with large, shadowed eyes, full lips, and a big nose.

I am also like my grandma in that we both tend to worry, which she is doing, I notice, as she eats bites of the lasagna. It's an exotic creation, with a blanket of sautéed carrots and another of sautéed eggplant laid down between the usual layers, and I think at first that our grandma is perturbed that Arthur has altered one of her specialties. Her large eyes seem larger and darker than usual, her brow is more furrowed, and even as she eats her lips are puckered in a sort of pout. She isn't speaking, but you have to speak quickly and loudly in our family if you want to be heard.

It's our habit to save the salad for last, and the whole table is quiet for a moment when we dig into our greens. During this moment of quiet, my grandma speaks. All I catch is, "So little respect."

"What? What did you say, Ma?" my dad asks.

"The way they talk to you—your sons," my grandma says. "My grandsons. The names they call you."

My dad squints and leans forward as he struggles to grasp what his mother is getting at; more than once he's said that he became a psychiatrist so that he could figure his mother out. "Oh, you mean calling me 'Old Man'? Are you worrying about that again, Ma? It's nothing, Ma. They're just fooling around."

Grandma doesn't answer right away. We are all watching her big, troubled eyes and her worried mouth. "You never spoke that way to your father," she says. The rest of us remain silent. My brothers and I have been calling our dad "Old Man" since we were teenagers. This is the first time that I, anyway, have heard our grandma object.

My mom breaks the silence cheerfully. "Times are different now, Mom. Kids joke more with their parents, and it isn't considered disrespectful."

"We don't mean anything by it, Grandma," Arthur says.

Our grandma shrugs. "He never in all his life spoke like that to his father."

"That's because my father was a full-blooded Sicilian," my dad says. "These punks think they can take advantage of me because

I'm only half Sicilian, but they're *wrong*." His arm flashes to his left and wraps around Zachary's head, then he pulls Zachary's huge head down to his armpit and begins clamping it rhythmically, mashing his tight curls, squeezing his cheekbones. Zachary submits; beneath our dad's forearm, he is grimacing or grinning.

My grandma looks at her son sorrowfully. "You never fought with your father, either."

"That's because I knew better than to pick a fight with a Sicilian."

"Oh, Ralph, how you talk. Your father was the gentlest man in all of Queens."

My mom speaks up again, trying to explain. "They're not being disrespectful, Mom. When they call him 'Old Man,' they mean it affectionately."

My grandma shrugs, unhappily. Michael, who is sitting next to her, drapes his arm across the back of her chair. "It's okay, Grandma, really it is. Remember when we used to have long hair, and we told you it was just the style? It's the same thing. This is just the style."

"Then why is Arthur's hair *still* long?" Grandma asks.

"Yeah, Arthur, what's *wrong* with you?" Dan says.

Arthur tips back his head. His straight, dark-blond hair is gathered into a long tail. "Hey, Dan," he says, "what's wrong with *you*?" Dan is almost as bald as our dad.

"Don't get disrespectful with me, pal," Dan says. "This is the style."

I wake in the night at the clicking of my grandma's rosary.

"Grandma, what's the matter?" I ask.

"Oh, I'm so sorry I woke you," she says.

I'm sharing a bed with my grandma because she's too old to sleep on a couch or on the floor and too small to need a double bed all for herself. It's Arthur's bed. Arthur has given the bed up for our grandma, and I guess I could feel lucky to be allotted the other half, but getting paired with our grandma reminds me that I have no true other half to sleep with and that I haven't had for some time.

"I'm so sorry I woke you," my grandma says again.

"That's okay, Grandma, I'm a light sleeper," I answer, thinking that if I'm going to be awakened in the middle of the night by someone lying next to me, I want it to be by a man—a man waking me up on purpose, wanting to do something more interesting than work a rosary.

"Are you worried about something, Grandma?" I ask.

"No," my grandma says, sounding mournful.

"Then why are you praying in the middle of the night?"

My grandma sighs. "To bore myself to sleep, God forgive me."

I turn away from her so she can't see my smile.

"I'm so sorry I woke you," she says again.

"That's okay, Grandma."

"I'll put it away now." I hear her rosary clacking and sliding onto the night table. She falls back to sleep before I do.

I lie awake thinking about Toby, wishing I'd said yes. Yes to lunch and to whatever else. He will be in Canada visiting relatives by tomorrow, so it's too late for me to change my mind. Of course, I think, breathing quietly on my side, I always change my mind when it's too late. There was a man who fell in love with me when Marly was a baby, and even though I had started to fall in love with him and my marriage was dying, I ran away from him, figuratively and almost literally—I hurried away down the street while Al followed me and spoke to me from the other side. This is crazy, I thought as I quickened my stride; I was on my way to Penney's to buy my husband and myself some socks, and I had a one-year-old baby at home waiting for me.

A year after Al followed me, calling to me, he became engaged to someone else; by the time I was free, he'd been remarried for several years.

At least I didn't tell Toby no, never—I said maybe we could meet for lunch after the holidays. Maybe I'd drive to the Detroit area without stopping to see my parents, or maybe he could meet me halfway across the state. He said he would like that very much and would see what we could arrange.

I wake again at the sound of my grandma's snoring. My grandma is so tiny that the shape of her almost disappears beneath the covers, yet she snores as loudly as a full-size person. I think of what my mom has told me about getting my dad to stop: first she tries nudging him with her elbow, next she pokes him with her finger, and if he still keeps it up, she barks out his name. "What?" he'll say. "Stop snoring," she'll order, and he'll fall back to sleep and be quiet for a while.

I lie on my back listening to my grandmother. Then I turn toward her face. Arthur has stuck a nightlight into the outlet over the bed, because when he wakes in the dark he sometimes forgets where he is, he thinks he is in one of the apartments or houses of his drug-addict years and that he is still an addict; with the light on, seeing our parents' old dresser draped with his clothes and his own artwork, his junk-shop Jesus art, and his nieces' drawings on the walls, he remembers where he is and doesn't panic.

Using drugs all those years has made him like a Vietnam veteran, I think: too much damage has occurred for the past to contain; it keeps leaking into the present. But maybe everybody's past is like that, it just leaks in more subtly. I wonder how much of my grandma's past still leaks or floats into her present. She seems too small to contain all the years she has lived. And in the light from Arthur's nightlight, which my grandma has switched on in case she has to get up to use the bathroom, she seems too fragile for me to touch, let alone elbow or poke.

Besides, if she wakes up she'll be mortified at having woken me again. She always makes such a big deal out of everything; when one of us catches a cold, even, she treats it like a calamity. She still talks about the loss of Dan's legs as if it happened last month, and when someone refers to mine or Dan's or Arthur's divorces, her face takes on the suffering look of Mary at the death of Jesus. She never gets over anything, not even halfway. Sometimes it seems that she doesn't even make an attempt. I love my grandma, but despite our resemblances, I'm very different from her. And as I stare at her lined and sunken cheeks (her teeth, a full set, are in a jar on the night table) I realize that, even though she held me when I was a baby and has hugged and kissed me every year of my life since, I don't know her well enough to touch her while she is sleeping.

I turn onto my back and, as my grandma snores, I pass the time by looking at Arthur's collection of junk-shop religious art. In deference to our grandma, Arthur has taken down the religious art that he has made himself, such as *The Last Breakfast*, in which Jesus and his disciples are consuming bananas, diet Coke, and Cap'n Crunch, but he has left up his less inflammatory ceramic wall sculptures, Greta's, Ruth's, and Marly's drawings, and a collection of religious kitsch that looks as if it has been lifted from the walls of our grandma's apartment.

Of four pieces, there are two crucifixes hanging high up in the shadows. (I'm thankful that, in the limited light of the nightlight, I can't see their dripping blood.) On the wall across the room is a print of Jesus walking on water with his unpierced hands at his sides and his smooth, broad feet just barely dimpling the water's surface. And closer to me, on the wall to my left, is a print of Jesus in which his heart has been pierced by thorns and risen to the surface of his chest. Jesus's heart is lying right on top of his skin or else the skin has disappeared; either way, his heart is exposed to the air. Thin yellow lines painted around it signify that it glows with an ethereal light, or that despite its being pierced and exposed it continues to beat. My grandma has told me that the heart is glowing and bleeding and exposed like that because Jesus loves us so much, but it makes me think of when I was a child visiting my grandmother and I slept in a room with a crucifix over the bed: my parents were raising us kids as atheists and I didn't know who Jesus was, and I was afraid that whoever had done that to that man would come in the night and get me.

Perhaps because of this memory, staring at the exposed heart makes me feel a little squeamish. I close my eyes to block it out. This magnifies the sound of my grandma's snoring, which reminds me of a death rattle except that it keeps starting up again. I know that I'll never fall back to sleep with that sound, so, gathering up my pillow and timing my exit with one of my grandma's snores, I slip from the bed and go out into the living room.

Halfway across the living room, I stop and stare out. The lights of the city and the darkness they shine in seem alive. The bright yellow lights shimmer and so does the liquid black air; it's as if I can see their molecules moving. If I open a window, it seems that I might hear sound—music, maybe, or humming.

Inside the living room the air is gray and sleepy, motionless and utterly quiet. The white couches glow faintly around the still forms of Arthur and Dan. Zach and Sasha are sleeping side by side on the floor. The rest of my family are paired off in other rooms: my parents in their own bed at the back of the apartment, Marly and Nicole on the floor of the computer room, and Mike and Sarah at the Renaissance Center, which towers like a black-and-gold fortress outside the windows, half a mile across the sky. Standing by myself in the middle of the living room, the only one up and awake, it seems that the pairs in the other rooms have floated off to other worlds, and even the ones within my sight seem as far beyond my reach as if they have fallen under a spell.

I scavenge the blanket that Dan has thrown off (his broad, compact body keeps itself warm) and lie down on the strip of carpet behind the couch next to the largest wall of windows; I lie on my back on the thick, padded carpet and look up and out at the black-and-yellow night and wonder where Toby is, and if he is awake. Probably he is sleeping. I want him awake and lying down with me, even though my strip of carpet is so narrow that my hand rests on its knotted fringe.

I haven't seen Toby in more than two years, yet I still remember the brush of his lips on my neck and the softness of his mouth as we kissed. I remember how soothing his arms felt around me, even though—stupidly, I think now—we remained standing. I want to lie down with him and feel the whole weight and length of him pressed hard against my body. I would remove my flannel nightgown. We wouldn't need one inch of extra space. And if we wanted more room and privacy, we could walk across the sky to the Renaissance Center and slip through a window onto a big, empty bed. I want to make love with Toby on a wide, blank bed without thinking about anyone else, and then I want to fall asleep with him, I want to feel his arms holding me and his skin against my skin as we drift off to the same place.

When I wake again, it's still night, but the darkness outside the windows seems quieter, and faded, and though it is quiet, too, inside the apartment, and from the stillness I can tell that my whole family is still asleep, they don't seem so far away from me anymore. I feel that if I call to any one of them they will wake right up and answer me. Maybe the only difference between now and before is that now the night is almost over, it's actually morning already. Soon we'll get up, one and two at a time, and sit around and eat breakfast and read the paper.

I'm drifting back to sleep again when it occurs to me that if my grandma wakes and finds me gone she'll want to know why I left her. I'll have to tell her the truth, or else make something up. I can say that the bed was too soft or the nightlight too bright, but chances are she won't believe me. She'll feel bad for having driven me off, and I'll feel bad for making her feel bad, and, on top of all this bad feeling, I'll have to listen to her apologize for the rest of the day.

I peel back my blanket and am about to get up from the floor when Dan calls to me from the other side of the couch: "Annie? Is that you?"

"Yeah."

I hear him scrambling and feel the couch moving a little; then a hand closes around my foot and feels its shape. "I thought you were Greta or Ruth at first," Dan says. "They're the ones who usually sneak up on me and steal my blankets."

"I didn't steal it," I say. "It was lying at the end of the couch."

"Yeah, sure."

"You can have it back."

"No, go ahead and keep it," Dan says. "I'm not cold."

"I don't need it anymore," I say. "I'm going back to the bed."

"Will you two be quiet?" Arthur calls from the other couch. "Annie, what are you doing out here anyway?"

"Grandma was snoring."

Arthur laughs.

"Yeah, you think it's funny, you try sleeping with her," I say.

"I'm trying to cut back on the number of women I sleep with," Arthur says.

"Well, I'd rather be sleeping with a man. Just one." *A certain one*, I think but don't add. I told Arthur and Dan a long time ago about meeting Toby, and they know that falling in love with him was the last thing I did before Ray asked me to leave our marriage and our house. I think of telling my brothers now about Toby's latest letter and asking them for advice. But I know that I'm not going to figure out what to do just yet, no matter what advice anyone gives me. I'm afraid of making the same mistake that I made by running away from Al, whom I can see now, from a distance of seven years, would have been a good husband for me. And I'm just as afraid of making the opposite mistake, as I did by getting involved with my lover from Grand Haven, who was not unhappily married, as I naively assumed, but only wanted a supplement to his marriage.

I set Dan's blanket on the arm of his couch, pick up my pillow, and start across the room.

"Ann," Dan calls, trying to catch me before I reach the hall.

I stop and turn back toward him.

"Want to go running tomorrow?" he asks. He means that I'll run and he'll wheel.

"I'm out of shape," I say. "I'd never keep up."

"You could borrow Mom's bike," Dan says. We've done this before; Dan gets a good workout, while I ride at a fairly leisurely pace.

"I don't know," I say. "I might be too tired."

"The cold air will wake you up," Dan says.

"I might be too beat. I haven't gotten much sleep tonight."

"All the more reason to get your butt out there," Dan says. "Fresh air and exercise are good for insomnia."

"Well, I'll see how I feel in the morning."

"You can hold onto the back of my chair and just coast," Dan says. "Or I'll wheel alongside you and turn the pedals with my hands. Or you can just junk the bike, and Zach will carry you on his back."

I laugh, imagining riding Zach horsey-back through the streets. "Okay," I say.

"The weather's supposed to stay mild," Dan says. "Above freezing, anyway. We'll go in the morning, when Mike and Sarah get back from the RenCen. They wanted to come, too."

"It's not going to be above freezing in the morning," Arthur says.

"Do you want to go, Arthur?" Dan asks.

"Nah," Arthur says.

"You could run," I say, thinking that if Arthur started to seize, we'd be there to cushion his fall and to help him home after it was over.

"I haven't run in years," Arthur says.

"You could borrow Dad's bike," I say.

"And his helmet," Dan says. "We could run around you, in formation."

"Maybe," Arthur says.

"We can run by those old warehouses between Jefferson and the river," Dan says. "There's hardly any traffic. We'll have the streets to ourselves."

"It sounds like it would be fun," Arthur says. "I'll think about it. I'll sleep on it."

I hug my pillow under my arm and walk back to Arthur's room and stop in the hallway and look in. The yellow light from the nightlight is bathing the walls with a soft glow and casting a bright circle on the bed. My grandma is lying on her side, facing the door. Her wrinkled face is still and her large eyes are closed.

I step around to the bed's far side, keeping my gaze lowered so I won't see the exposed heart, and lift the covers and slip in, and as the blankets settle over me with their soothing, protective weight, I try not to think about Toby for now.

But as soon as I close my eyes, he appears in my vision; I see him as he looked more than two years ago, during the last half hour of the conference. He is sitting across from me at the small table in his room, wearing khaki pants and a maroon corduroy shirt. He isn't looking at me. His hands are shaking. In another second our conversation will falter, and he'll stand up and walk to me and ask me to stand, too, and I'll soar with the possibility, opening as suddenly as our mouths, of us being together in the future.

I try not to feel that hope now. It's been over two years since I've even seen Toby's face, and though in his last letter he said he'd like to arrange to meet me again, in his first letter he warned me: *Don't make any plans that have me in them, Annie, because you'll only hurt yourself to imagine them.* Something has changed for him since then, but I don't know what has changed or how much, and whatever it is that is different now, I'm afraid that his first words are still true—that my plans with him in them will not become real.

I turn onto my side on my half of the bed and try to turn my thoughts away from him again; I think of how, in a couple of hours, I'll get up and get dressed and ride my mother's bike down by the old warehouses, with Dan, and maybe Arthur, and Mike, Sarah, and Zach. And as I curl up on my side, looking forward to the coming morning, imagining the gray, rippling surface of the river and the grimy walls and dark windows of the old warehouses, sleep drifts toward me once more, loosening my body and my breath. I open my eyes and close them again, taking in with me the soft glow of the room and my grandmother breathing quietly beside me.

The Iowa Short Fiction Award and John Simmons Short Fiction Award Winners

1997
Thank You for Being Concerned and Sensitive, Jim Henry
Judge: Ann Beattie

1997
Within the Lighted City,
Lisa Lenzo
Judge: Ann Beattie

1996
Hints of His Mortality,
David Borofka
Judge: Oscar Hijuelos

1996
Western Electric, Don Zancanella
Judge: Oscar Hijuelos

1995
Listening to Mozart,
Charles Wyatt
Judge: Ethan Canin

1995
May You Live in Interesting Times, Tereze Glück
Judge: Ethan Canin

1994
The Good Doctor,
Susan Onthank Mates
Judge: Joy Williams

1994
Igloo among Palms,
Rod Val Moore
Judge: Joy Williams

1993
Happiness, Ann Harleman
Judge: Francine Prose

1993
Macauley's Thumb,
Lex Williford
Judge: Francine Prose

1993
Where Love Leaves Us,
Renée Manfredi
Judge: Francine Prose

1992
My Body to You,
Elizabeth Searle
Judge: James Salter

1992
Imaginary Men, Enid Shomer
Judge: James Salter

1991
The Ant Generator,
Elizabeth Harris
Judge: Marilynne Robinson

1991
Traps, Sondra Spatt Olsen
Judge: Marilynne Robinson

1990
A Hole in the Language,
Marly Swick
Judge: Jayne Anne Phillips

1989
Lent: The Slow Fast,
Starkey Flythe, Jr.
Judge: Gail Godwin

1989
Line of Fall, Miles Wilson
Judge: Gail Godwin

1988
The Long White,
Sharon Dilworth
Judge: Robert Stone

1988
The Venus Tree,
Michael Pritchett
Judge: Robert Stone

1987
Fruit of the Month, Abby Frucht
Judge: Alison Lurie

1987
Star Game, Lucia Nevai
Judge: Alison Lurie

1986
Eminent Domain, Dan O'Brien
Judge: Iowa Writers' Workshop

1986
Resurrectionists,
Russell Working
Judge: Tobias Wolff

1985
Dancing in the Movies,
Robert Boswell
Judge: Tim O'Brien

1984
Old Wives' Tales,
Susan M. Dodd
Judge: Frederick Busch

1983
Heart Failure, Ivy Goodman
Judge: Alice Adams

1982
Shiny Objects, Dianne Benedict
Judge: Raymond Carver

1981
The Phototropic Woman,
Annabel Thomas
Judge: Doris Grumbach

1980
Impossible Appetites,
James Fetler
Judge: Francine du Plessix Gray

1979
Fly Away Home, Mary Hedin
Judge: John Gardner

1978
A Nest of Hooks, Lon Otto
Judge: Stanley Elkin

1977
The Women in the Mirror,
Pat Carr
Judge: Leonard Michaels

1976
The Black Velvet Girl,
C. E. Poverman
Judge: Donald Barthelme

1975
*Harry Belten and the
Mendelssohn Violin Concerto,*
Barry Targan
Judge: George P. Garrett

1974
*After the First Death There Is No
Other,* Natalie L. M. Petesch
Judge: William H. Gass

1973
The Itinerary of Beggars,
H. E. Francis
Judge: John Hawkes

1972
The Burning and Other Stories,
Jack Cady
Judge: Joyce Carol Oates

1971
Old Morals, Small Continents,
Darker Times,
Philip F. O'Connor
Judge: George P. Elliott

1970
The Beach Umbrella,
Cyrus Colter
Judges: Vance Bourjaily and
Kurt Vonnegut, Jr.